The Barn

J. Richard Wakefield

Signalman Publishing

The Barn
by J. Richard Wakefield

Signalman Publishing
www.signalmanpublishing.com
email: info@signalmanpublishing.com
Kissimmee, Florida

ISBN:
978-1-940145-52-5 (paperback)
978-1-940145-53-2 (ebook)

Signalman
Publishing

Also by J. Richard Wakefield

Blinding White Flash

Blinding White Flash: Invasion

Dedicated to my nine grandchildren.
May this be a legacy to make them proud.

Acknowledgments

I wish to thank the following for helping me write this book.

The London Writers Group: Ruth Zavitz, Pat Brown, Clarissa Harwood, John Jeneroux, Ian Gillespie, Mitch Lenko and Carl Zvonkin. Throughout the past eight years, these people have been instrumental in honing my writing skills.

Also, Christopher McGarry, for his editing and proof reading.

Finally my family: Jeremy, Charaxes, Jennifer, Brent, and most of all, my loving wife Dorothy for their helpful input and patience.

I was abducted

The man woke up into total darkness.

Normally, his bedroom had a nightlight, in case he had to get up for one of his children during the night. Even without the nightlight, at least a streetlight would peer through their window. But nothing.

He never wakes up in the middle of the night, unless it's for one of his children having a bad dream. But there was no sound.

Why is it so dark? Why can't I see anything?

He couldn't even see his hand in front of his face. Nothing. His eyes were open. But it's just black.

He realized: *Hey, this isn't my bed. It's some kind of bunk, or a table.*

It was hard, with a bare thin foam mattress. He was covered with a thin blanket, not his duvet.

He felt light headed. He also had a mild stabbing pain in the small of his back. He was definitely not home.

He tried to get up, but was startled at the sound of metal rattling, piercing the silence that enveloped him.

What's around my neck?

He felt a thick metal band circumventing his neck. It was bolted on the right, and bolted on the left. A chain was secured to the collar. He followed it with his fingers. The shackle ended in a hole in the wall on the left side above him.

It's well secured. He tried to pull on it, but it wouldn't budge.

He was dizzy, and confused.

Where in Christ am I?

He got up, stumbling a bit, taking two attempts to get to his feet. The floor was cold on his bare feet. It was concrete, with scattered straw and dirt.

Clearly he wasn't home. He tried to remember. But nothing came to him except a headache and the dizziness. He sat back down, hurting his buttocks on the lip of the bed.

Oh, right, my watch. It glows in the dark. I can get the time and date.

But his two thousand dollar gold Bulgari was not on his arm. He felt for his cell phone, but there was no night table, and his clothing had no pockets. He was getting frustrated and confused.

"Yvonne!" The expected reply didn't come. Nothing but the silence. "Yvonne, are you there?" He listened carefully. But, nothing.

The man started to get panicky. Sweat beaded on his forehead, dripping down burning his eyes. A cold clammy feeling encased him. He was getting nauseated. His heart was pounding, and he was breathing quickly.

What the hell is going on? Where in Christ am I?

"HELLO! ANYBODY THERE?"

Nothing.

But there, in the distance, he could see a faint glow, small, and rectangular. Definitely a faint glow.

He stood up, the chain rattled, piercing the silence again. There was a sharp pain in his back, stabbing, burning sting of a mild amplitude.

Ok, Ok. Calm down. Deep breaths.

He pondered his past events to piece things together.

Ok, what's the last thing I remember? I was in my office. It was late, after 10:00pm. I was finishing up the Ohio Mutual file. Deadline is tomorrow. I went to my car to head home. Damn, I don't remember anything after that.

Then he realized, a sinking feeling of helplessness.

"Holy shit! That's not going to happen! I'll miss that meeting!"

"ANY BODY THERE? HELLO!"

Nothing. He realized he felt like Tom Hanks in Cast Away.

Stupid. Why would I even think about that?

He remembered. He was about to get in his car. Then searing pain in his back. Now he was here. He couldn't remember anything else.

Yes, I've been kidnapped.

But why? He wondered if he was going to be a sex toy. Maybe some snuff video. Maybe they want his organs to sell them to the highest bidder. He'd never experienced such fear in his life. Again, panic started to seep into him, like being smothered in hot tar.

Christ, I wonder if they took my family too? Are they here? "HELP! Anyone there?" *I gotta get out of here.*

He had to get this chain off the wall.

"PULL! PULL! AAAAAAHHH! Move you fucker! Move! Jesus Christ!"

As hard as he tried, it didn't move, not even a creak. It was well secured on the other side of the wood wall. He wasn't going anywhere. His hands felt raw and sore.

Totally spent, and still wobbly, he laid back down on the make-shift bed.

It was uncomfortable. He couldn't find a restful position. Flat on his back was not as bad.

Now, think, think. What the hell is going on here?

He wondered. Was he kidnapped for ransom? Were some fuckers trying to steal his money?

Man, someone is going to pay for this! They won't get away with it. No way.

But who? Who the in hell would want to kidnap him? Yvonne? No, why would his wife want him gone? Shit, maybe she did want him gone. He had a huge insurance policy. No, she would never do that to him. Would she? No. He didn't believe it. She loved him.

Ah, there was De Luca. Now he was a real piece of work. But his worth was much more than the man, so why would he want the man's money?

No, Roberto wouldn't do this to me, we've been friends far too long. We've done too much together.

So, who?

No one at work could pull this off, he thought. Must be more than one person. A conspiracy. It's gotta be someone outside. People he didn't know maybe. Someone who found him on the Internet? He didn't know. It didn't matter, even if he did figure it out. Who would he be able to tell?

He lay there with empty thoughts. Then he remembered. He recalled seeing a bit of a TV show where someone was handcuffed to a roof of a building. That person got away by cutting off his hand. Animals caught in traps would gnaw off their ensnared limb to get away. He wouldn't be able to cut off his head though.

Christ I'm tired. Thirsty too. Damn thirsty.

He couldn't find a comfortable position because of the damn chain.

He felt around the bed in the dark.

"Damn! Shit!"

He got a splinter in his finger. The thick lumber wasn't finished. He managed to get the sliver out with his teeth. He couldn't see the puncture, but tasted blood.

The wall also felt like thick wood. He wondered, *could he touch the ceiling? Ah, there, just about out of reach.* He could feel the thick beams running long the ceiling. But he couldn't quite reach the floor above.

He wondered, *could he reach that glow?* He got out of bed and crawled through the darkness. He didn't want to trip over something.

Jesus, the floor is cold and dirty. "Damn it!"

The chain came to an end very quickly. How far was that? He tried standing, which was difficult in the depressing black. So, three steps back to the bed. He was on a short leash.

He decided to check each side. He felt a table just to his front right. It was solid wood. He gave it a pull. It wouldn't budge. Likely bolted to the wall.

What's this?

He felt a large container, which seemed to be filled with water. He opened it and smelled. Yep, it was water.

Groping he found two loaves of bread. Then a heavy plastic jar. He opened it. Peanut butter, he could smell it. There was another plastic jar, which, when opened, smelled like jam. He stuck his finger into it. Just like he did when he was a little kid.

It was jam. Strawberry jam. The only other object there was a plastic knife. Must be one of those you get at McDonalds. The food confirmed he'd been kidnapped, likely for ransom.

Am I going to be here a while? The food and water seems to indicate that. Maybe it's just in case.

He tried the left side. A small wall was at the end of the bed. A large wooden box was on the floor on the opposite side of the wall. It was several feet across and chair height. The man felt around the top. There was some kind of lid, made of wood with a handle of wood. It was just sitting on the box. The lid was loose covering a hole in the top of the box. A hole the size of a toilet.

He sighed, "Gotta be. Fucking great."

Beyond the makeshift toilet, he felt a solid concrete wall. It was just about out of his reach.

I'm tired as hell. Nothing I can do about this. Might as well get back to bed. He stumbled back in the dark, the chain getting in his way. He stubbed his right toe on the base of the wall at the end of the bed.

Once prone, he just pulled the cover over him. Maybe this was some dream. But he couldn't sleep. He gazed at the black for hours, his mind tossing around thoughts.

My family must be going crazy, he wondered. *Do they even know*

I'm missing? Maybe they've been taken too.

A dreaded thought. *Maybe they're dead.* "Oh, Christ no!"

"Oh, God, please have my family safe, please. I beg you, please. Please, get me out of here."

His mind wondered back to his work. He was worried sick about what was going to happen with his business. How's it going to survive? Who's going to make the crucial decisions? Who's going to hold client's hands? He ran that company like a ship's captain.

It's my life's wro…

"Nick. Are you going to deliver your report on time?"

"Oh, yes. It will be completed tomorrow, you'll be very pleased with the results."

"That report is going to show our clients what we want them to see about us, right. Like we discussed before?"

"Yes. You do understand the data doesn't support your premise."

"I understand, we're well aware of that. We're working on that problem. You do a good job for us, I can guarantee we'll sign more contracts in the future."

He woke to a golden beam shining in his eyes. The sun's light was coming through the far window. Just like home.

That was some scary dream.

Then he realized it was no dream. As he moved, the chain rattled, and he realized he wasn't in his bed. He looked around to get his first vision of his cell.

"Oh, shit! I *am* chained to the wall," he screeched.

With the sun so low shining through the window, it must have been just after dawn.

He had an important meeting at 10am today, provided it was the next day. Anger and frustration streamed through his body.

I'll lose hundreds of thousands on this.

That client needed major handholding. It was a crucial meeting. "FUCK!"

Yvonne must have called the police by now, he thought. Surely they were looking for him.

He was hungry.

I missed having breakfast with my kids. My kids, they must be worried sick. I need to get out of here.

He needed to test how the chain was secured. He studied the wall it went though. A hole was freshly drilled through the thick lumber. The chain just cleared through the orifice, being secured on the far side.

Christ, that's never going to give. No way I'm going to get that out.

Then he remembered. The God damned market was tanking yesterday. It was down two percent when he left the office. He was losing money all over. It still infuriated him when he'd lost a million dollars when the housing bubble collapsed two years ago. It was times like that he didn't want to be reminded of his losses, like when he lost hundreds of thousands when Nortel collapsed. Now this! "FUCK!"

He was shaking again. He was scared shitless.

God damnit, I need to get out of here. "Pull! Pull!"

The chain was well secured. He tried kicking it. "Ouch! Damn it."

He hurt the bottom of his foot. "FUCK!"

"My money… My family…"

He started to sob uncontrollably. He hadn't sobbed like that since his grandmother died recently. There's no tissue for his nose. It dripped on his shirt mixing with tears. It was gross.

Ok, what do we have here?

He was dressed in red plaid pyjama pants, and matching plaid shirt. He had no socks, and no underwear.

He looked around the room. It was much longer than wide by twice as much. There was a new steel door at the far right corner. It was way beyond his reach.

The best he could do was a quarter across the room.

The room looked like some kind of old horse stall, like he'd seen in movies. The concrete walls, one on his left, the other in front with the window, had old white-wash, mostly flaking off. He guessed those were foundations, maybe, sure looked thick enough.

The wooden walls were rough cut, and well aged. He wondered if he could pick away at the wood. But, they looked too thick, and were also hardwood.

The floor was concrete, with small smatters of faded grey paint. Straw and dirt was scattered around. It accumulated as small hills at the four corners.

What about the ceiling? He wondered if he could get through that.

Hmm, even if I can get the chain out of the wall, I doubt I'm going to get through the top.

The ceiling was large beams, mostly untrimmed logs. Boards were on top of them forming another floor above. Lengths of straw drooped down through cracks between the boards.

The table with water and jars of food was fresh made, screwed to the wall with metal brackets, but no legs. It was about eighteen inches wide, and some four foot long.

Curious, at the far end of the table on the wall was a steel plate. He pondered if he could poke around at it with his fingers it might move. But it wouldn't budge. A door? It was too small to crawl through.

He was hungry. He ate four slices of the whole wheat bread, covered with jam and peanut butter. But afterwards he was still hungry and thirsty. He swallowed it down with some water. It was awful.

Peanut butter and jam is for kids. Yvonne makes that for the kids. *I'll bet they had that this morning. And I wasn't there...*

It wasn't his normal breakfast of bacon and eggs, or sausage and scrambled eggs. He missed his morning orange juice. He missed his morning coffee.

Hmm, coffee....

I miss going to work. Work... I feel sick again.

How does someone follow time in a place like this?

The smell was like horseshit. Maybe pig shit. He remembered the stench from when a new client took him to an agriculture fair one year. He gagged so much there he couldn't even eat a lunch. But he toughed it out to get the contract. It reminded him of why he couldn't stand the country.

Too open for me. No people. I like people. Lots of people.

Lots of people means money to be made.

"Jesus Christ! God, where are you? Why have you let this happen to me?"

God was testing him. That's what this must be about.

What's that?

Sounded like a car. Far in the distance, but definitely a car.

"HEY! I'm in here! Help me please!"

It was gone.

The sun stopped shining through the window. Sitting on the edge of the bed, he watched it creep along the floor away from him. Then it vanished. Must be afternoon. No meeting. No money.

Maybe my father picked up the slack. George would for sure. He's reliable. He knows people. That's why I made him second in command last year. That was a good call on my part.

He knew talent when he saw it. He'd had to let people go who don't show talent. Nothing personal, of course, just business.

They'll come through on the Ohio Mutual file, he thought.

The kidnappers must have gotten through to his wife by now.

Oh, my wife. I sure hope Yvonne can get me out of here. My kids must be going crazy. Fuck, what if she's behind this? No, not Yvonne. I give her such a good life of luxury. Definitely much better than when I first met her. I still remember our first love.

But the though got trumped by another emotion.

"Christ, I'm hungry, and thirsty. I have to piss in the worst way. But that hole. FUCK!"

No choice. What a relief it was. The first tinkle at the bottom took a bit, it must have been a deep hole. He couldn't see down to the bottom, it was too dark.

Guess that's all for dinner too. He was going to have to eat the peanut butter and jam on bread, and wash it down with water. Breakfast, lunch and dinner. That was a depressing thought.

How long is this going to last? No more than a couple days I hope.

He realized, he was going to have to wash with this water too.

The light disappeared. It certainly was black here at night. He'd never experienced such darkness. And still no one came. Silence was his only companion, along with the beating of his own heart in his ears. He was hungry again, but down to one loaf, plus half the water was gone.

I better conserve.

Yvonne and I are in the living room watching TV. Someone's in the room with us. 'Who is this?" I ask.

"He's my trainer."

Wow, what a body and so strong. I turn to him. "Get out."

"No, I'm here to train her."

"Get the fuck out or I'll throw you..."

Rumble.

The man woke.

What's that? Oh, just thunder.

It was refreshing to see the odd lightning flash stream into his room, breaking up the absolute black, even if only for a brief moment. He wasn't going to be able to sleep with the noise. He needed quiet to sleep. Yet, that was all he had in here, yet no quiet for him to sleep tonight.

His joints ached lying on this bed. It was so uncomfortable. The chain was pinching him when he was forced to lay on it.

Christ, I'm thirsty. Gotta pee again.

He waited for a flash so he could aim for the hole. Of course, he had to miss and pissed all over the top of the box.

"Ouch!" *Hell. Fuck that hurts.*

He stubbed his small toe, again, same place on the wall, while getting back in bed. So now that throbbing added to the discomfort lying there. He wouldn't be able to get back to sleep. He just lay there watching the flashes of light dance around the room. He even counted the seconds for the thunder, trying to remember the timing and distance that represented. Occasionally, the flash and crash was simultaneous. It startled him.

I should be in my own bed. I should be able to piss in my own throne. "FUCK!"

Drip, drip, drip, drip. It woke him.

It stopped raining. The only sound was the drips falling into small puddles from the ceiling. No sun on the floor, it was overcast outside. *I'm still here.*

Better not drink too much water or it'll be gone, he thought. He needed to keep track.

I could be here a while.

It dawned on him. *Oh, I know. I'll use some of this straw. I'll mark each day with a length of it in a crack in the wall above the table.*

This was day three, so three of them in a row. Yep, they stayed put. Great, now he could track the days.

There hadn't been anything all day, except quiet and his thoughts. He could hear something scurrying over his head, on the floor above.

*Great, mice. That's all I need. I hate vermin. Disgusting, dirty
creatures. God made them to piss us off.*

That was five straws today. It must be Sunday. He'd missed Mass.
His family was at church right now without the man present. He
could pray.

"Oh God. My Lord, Creator of the Universe. Please do not
forsake me. Please guide those who are looking for me. Answer
their prayers. Tell them where I am. You have infinite wisdom.
Infinite compassion. Please set me free from my bondage."

He had nothing but his arm to wipe his tears on.

All the food was gone. Water was done yesterday. The man was
hungry and thirsty. What's the point in getting up? He needed to do
some exercises. The man used to run at least three times a week.
Push-ups. Yeah, he could do a couple dozen of those. But he
couldn't make a baker's dozen, laying exhausted nose down on the
floor.

Taking a dump was hard. He had constipation, and no water to
wash with, wonderful. No toilet paper either, Christ, he thought.

He inserted the sixth straw this morning. It was raining again. It
had rained all day, heavier this time. High winds were hammering
a tree against the building. Water was dipping from the cracks in the
floor above. But, of course, it was out of his reach. He tried earlier
to stretch his hand as far as it could go but the chain pulled back. He
was inches away from the drip. Frustrated, he gave up.

He understood how dogs pulling on a leash felt.

Thirst was over powering.

I'm so fucking thirsty. "God, please let it drip in my reach."

By near end of the day, with the light fading, and the rain still coming down, a drip hit him in the face as he lay in bed. Water!

"Thank you God!"

He let it pool in his hands. It took a while, as the drips were not often. It didn't look clean, but he's gotta drink something. He spit it out.

"FUCK! It tastes like shit! Goddamn it!"

If I don't drink something I'm going to dehydrate. I gotta try it anyway. Probably make me sick. That's all I need, dysentery.

It tasted awful, but he sucked up as much as he could from his cupped palms.

He pondered; *Maybe I'm being punished. God is punishing me. But why?*

He lay on the floor, having to move the mattress off the bed as the dripping increased. Why would God punish him like this? He had nothing else to think about. At least it took his mind off the hunger, he thought.

His mind wandered to his previous life, recalling his path, trying to ignore the complaints from his stomach.

He was successful business wise, having built a business from scratch from long hours, and hard work. Though his motto was; work smart not hard.

God wants us to be successful. I made my own business with my own two hands.

He supplied a vital service to the insurance industry. He's been at it for more than ten years. Sure he had some down times. Who didn't? He even got sued once for firing someone. That hurt. Bastard sued him and the man lost. Fucking courts.

He was successful with his family.

I've been a good father and a good husband. I've provided. That's what I'm supposed to do. "Isn't that right, God?" he said looking up at the ceiling, but gazing beyond.

Business hadn't been great since the 2008 crash, but it had been slowly improving. His business had been growing again. *That's all good, right?*

I go to church, when I can. Unless I have to take a client golfing. Have to impress new clients. God understands. I pray, maybe not as often as I should. But my wife makes sure the kids pray, that should be good enough.

The steel collar was chaffing the man's neck. And his back ached. It even hurt to do sit ups. That wasn't good. Better stop exercising. He was burning a lot of calories.

They're going to bring more food, right? I'm going to starve to death here. I won't see my family again. I won't see my children again. I won't get to see any grandchildren.

The last of the light reminded him of the movie where the whole thing was in a coffin. He couldn't remember the film's title. It must feel the same as this, being in total darkness and confined. Depression overcame him.

Drip, drip, drip, drip…

More drips finding their way through the cracks woke the man. The rain had not let up. And it was colder.

All he had been wearing the past six days were the plaid pyjamas. He was starting to stink. He wasn't used to this. He used to shower every day. Brushing his teeth after every meal, three times a day. Now nothing. His mouth tasted the same as this fucking place, *SHIT!*

Varoom!

What's that? Another car. Way off, again. But now gone. The only remaining sound was the rain, and the dripping on the floor. A pool was forming at the far corner.

"Christ, I'm hungry."

How long can someone last without food? Without water? He had a massive headache. Shit, not even any Tylenol.

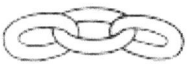

"Oh, daddy, thank you so much for the dolly. I love her!"

"You're most welcome, Angie. Do you know how old you are?"

"I'm three."

"That's right," Yvonne says. "Good girl, you're so smart."

"Let's blow out the candles now," I say.

"Happy birthday to you, happy birthday to you. Happy birthday, dear Angie. Happy birthday to you."

"Now blow!"

Clangk!

"What?"

"Such a big blow, Angel. Very goo..."

Clangk!

What was that? The man couldn't see, it was darker than black. Sounded like that little steel door. He felt along the table to that metal door at the far end of the table. "YES!" It had moved to almost the edge, like a tray.

Food???

Yes! He felt a large heavy container, same as the water jug.

"More water! Thank you, God."

There were two loaves of bread. He ripped one open and devoured half of it. Oh, man bread never tasted so good! He washed it down with some water.

"Hmm, that was wonderful."

Then he realized. *This may have to last a week again. How's someone supposed to live off this?* "FUCK!" He didn't even feel if there was more peanut butter and jam. Was there? He felt around. There it was. He couldn't remember where he put the McDonald's knife. He just scooped the jam with two fingers and shoved it into his mouth.

"Man, fantastic!"

Then he paused. His stomach didn't feel too good. *Burp!* "Oh, shi…." Hack! Spit! Hurl!

He puked, but where he couldn't see.

"Blaa, cough! Ptew!"

It didn't take long for the warmth on his feet to turn cold.

"Oh, God, I've puked on my feet."

His mouth was also burning from the acid.

That would leave a mess. It was going to stink too. So much for stuffing his face too fast. What a waste of food. He realized he was not going to have enough for the week should he be there that much longer.

I've gotta get out of here. He thought over and over. But that chain. "I've got to get it off the wall."

He grabbed the chain with both hands, with his butt on the bed, and both feed straddling the chain's receptacle on the wall. With all his might…"Pull! Pull! Common! Fucking break! Arg! Pull! Common! Aaaaa. MOVE!"

"I WANT TO GO HOME!… I want to go home. … Please, let me go home," he whimpered.

"I need to get out of here."

His heart was racing like crazy. It wanted to jump out of the man's chest. He was sweating profusely, a cold clammy sweat.

I've got to get home. I'm going to die here. "Christ, let me out of here!"

I've never been so scared in my life.

Not even that accident he had when he was racing that guy and totalled his car when he was young. That was scary. But this was an order of magnitude of fear beyond that.

"Shit, now I have to…"

Pfttt!

"Ugh, that fart stinks. Oh, shit…"

He just made it to the toilet. Great, now he had the shits, likely from that sewer water from above.

At least sitting there, on his excuse for a throne, he calmed down a bit. But his gut ached, with hard pain, relieved only when his bowel contents explosively splattered under him.

He stood, but felt a warm drip down the inside of his thigh.

Guess there was no point in trying the chain again. No way it was going to budge.

He felt around the wall where the metal plate was, maybe he could get it to move. No, the tray disappeared into the wall, with another plate of metal on the far side of the wall. "Humpf!" as he pressed hard on it. Nothing moved.

Maybe they're still there. I didn't hear anyone walking around though.

"Hey you there!! Anybody there!! Let me out. PLEASE let me the Christ out of here!"

Nothing. Not even any more dripping.

Let's see, ten, eleven, that was the twelfth straw in the crack this morning. The food was all gone, again. And only a small bit of water remained in the jug. The man had the shits earlier, again. *That fucking rain water.* He must have gone four times today, but only a small bit of fluid came out. Made the room just stink. His asshole burned because he couldn't wipe his ass. He tried to use the bread plastic bag. Didn't work well. He didn't think he had anything left in him to shit out, but more did come, for most of the morning.

He was expelling more fluid than he was taking in.

His fingernails were also getting long. No way of cutting them. He hated it when they got long. It was so un-groomed letting them get too long. The only way was to use his teeth. Disgusting that was. No way his hands were clean.

His toenails were also getting long. But he couldn't use his teeth to cut those. He realized he had cut his fingernails first so no way to trim the toenails with his fingernails.

Plus his balls were getting sore.

God damned rash starting between my legs because I can't shower.

He realised, he had a choice, fucking awful, use the last of the water to clean his butt or drink it. Yeah, there's no toilet paper, was a stark reminder.

"I find you guilty. Guilty of ignoring your family," the judge orders.

"But your honour, I work long days, seven days a week. How can I provide for my family, who I love very much..."

Klangk! Klank!

He woke. That was the tray again! Going back into the wall, and then back onto the table.

Must be my next food delivery.

He made his way in the dark to the table and felt around.

"Yes!" It was. Now, let's not make the same mistake, he thought. He had a bit of bread, swallowing it down with a small amount of water. Might as well go back to asleep, he thought.

I'll eat some of my special delivery in the morning.

It's a long walk, I've been at it for hours. The woods are thick with trees, I can't see far into them. But I recognize this place. I'm a very long way from home.

That opening ahead I can see the city. But it's so far away. I'll never be able to walk it.

Every step I take the trees surround me and the city gets further away. There's not a person anywhere to be seen.

He reluctantly woke. Lying on his side, he opened one eye. He looked around the pale lit room as the sun tried to come in. It no longer shone in his eyes. He gazed at the table of food. His stomach complained about the emptiness.

Ok, let's check my food inventory.

Same on his buffet as every time so far. Bread, jug full of water. Peanut butter, and jam. Oh, but look at this! A treat this time. A length of klobassa, about six inches long. That won't last.

"Let's have that first. To hell with cutting it with the knife."

He seized a big bite at the end to try to get the plastic off. Took a bit of work, and numerous spits of small plastic, but there it was. He took a mouthful.

Hmmm, wow, that's fantastic, he thought. No, not all of it, he paused. "Let's let this extravagance last."

Chewing bread, with peanut butter and jam, he looked at the wall with his count of days. One, two, three… thirteen. He inserted the fourteenth straw. Two weeks. Yeah, this morning's was fourteen straws in the wall. The number cried out. He'd been here two weeks. Despair replaced his hunger.

He finished one slice of bread and washed it down with a small bit of water.

"Man, I'm hungry again. But I guess I'm going to have to ration this delivery. I need to make it last a week."

His heart sunk. This food meant he was going to be here another week, at least. Panic started to set in again. He couldn't control it. He screamed. He yelled. He broke out in a tantrum.

He needed to get control of himself. He couldn't keep going on a tirade like this. He needed to stop. He was consuming too much energy. He tried to think of something else. But the thought of food was hard to push aside.

We used to get Chinese food delivered at work on late sessions, he thought trying to calm down. Funny, why he would think that now. He missed Chinese food.

"Mr. Easton, this is the Illinois State Police. Can you hear us?"

What? I've been found! "Yes, I'm here. Please get me out!"

"We will, Mr. Easton. We need to cut the door to get it open. Stand back."

They're cutting the door. I've been rescued! My family! My business!

Clangk!

What? Oh, Christ, he was just dreaming. *Was that another food drop?* He thought for a bit. *It couldn't be, could it? One was yesterday.* He felt around the table, everything was where he left it. Nothing new. Disappointed he went back to bed not understanding what the sound was which woke him. He so much wanted that dream to be reality. He lay there trying to remember the dream, but it faded as he drifted off.

In the morning, like a robot, he went to the table, and made his meal of the day. He ate it sitting at the side of the bed, while staring at nothing.

He got up to his calendar of days.

"One, two, three, four, five, seven, eight. Shit, five, SIX, seven, eight, nine, ten, eleven, twelve, thirteen, fourteen. And this one makes fifteen. I've been here fifteen days."

He didn't understand. How long is this going to take? Surely they must have made a deal with the kidnappers by now, he thought.

Christ! Maybe something went wrong. Maybe they got killed and didn't tell the cops where he was. "FUCK, I'm going to die in this shit hole!"

He had no choice. He couldn't stand his own stench any longer. He had to wash. He just had to use some of his drinking water to wash his butt. He ripped a bit from the bottom of his pants and used that to wash his crotch. He realized, if he ripped another from the other leg he could make a toothbrush. If he didn't, he was going to lose teeth.

After cleaning himself as best he could, using as little water as possible, he laid naked on the bed looking up, gazing beyond the floor above. My business must be going down the toilet too, I'm not there, he thought.

Bet it's gone bankrupt, or going bankrupt. And what about my stocks? I have no idea what the market is doing. It was tough the last two years. I had to stay on it daily. Now I'm losing money.

He realized he was also losing his family.

My family, my money, and my business, my life. Lost.

Then he remembered, "At least I have my stash. If I can get out of here, I'll have enough to live on for a while until I get back on my feet."

He'd done it before. Every successful businessman had a long string of failures. He'd had his throughout the years. He remembered Donald Trump also came back from the brink, so could he. The thought calmed him a bit. He even relished at the challenge.

God damn it. That was a great dream he just had, he thought. He was in Paris with clients. He dined on caviar, steak and red wine.

Christ, I just had to wake up to the reality of my prison.

He'd had that, and similar dreams, many times. Each morning he woke from those dreams he got even more depressed.

Though, he didn't feel like crying today. Not like the last few days. Must have been at least once a day. Does no good of course.

He was so tired, so deep in sleep, he didn't even hear the delivery of food last night. It was there waiting for him. That's three weeks, twenty straws on the wall. Today will be day twenty-one.

It dawned on him. There are too many straws in a row. Of course, he hadn't planned to be here this long.

Oh, I know. I'll organize the straws into fives today.

He finished with some pride. There that's better. Easier to count. This was day twenty-one. Three weeks. More food means another week. Another - fucking - week.

The man ran out of water before the next delivery because he washed his ass, which used up too much water. He managed to use one of the peanut butter jars to catch drops of water when it rained couple days ago. He cringed having to wash himself with stinking water, Christ.

Then an epiphany, he remembered that urine was sterile when it first comes out. He recalled seeing it in a movie or TV show, or something. So, maybe if he pissed on his cloth then he could wash his ass with that, he thought.

"Let's try it."

He peed on a bit of his cloth, then used it to wash between his cheeks.

"Christ, that's gross. What a stench. Think I'm going to puke. Now I'm going to stink of urine." He did his best to keep his meagre food down.

He sat naked at the side of the bed, shivering in the cool damp air. The room was definitely getting stuffy. He craved fresh air.

Each food delivery came every week, like clockwork, like a ghost in the night. No one talks to me, he thought. The straws now count forty-nine. Seven weeks. Must be near November, getting cold enough in here to be November.

He tried his best to keep wrapped in the blanket.

This meant he missed Halloween with his kids. But then again, he'd missed it before. Business.

"Gotta do what I gotta do to provide for my family," he crowed.

He realized he was getting weaker. He could definitely feel it.

"I can only do half a dozen push-ups now," he lamented. "I have to save my strength. The food keeps coming, so there has to be some kind of progress on my case. They can't have forgotten me. Wonder what's taking so long." He felt down again, under the weight of a huge slab.

He missd his former life. At night, he kept dreaming of his past. He'd rather live in his dreams than this reality. He spent a lot of time lying in bed trying to dream. It was the only way to pass the long days, longer than he had ever experienced. He was used to not having enough hours in the day to get things done, often worked ten or twelve hour work days, which flew by. But now, each hour of nothing was agonizingly prolonged.

The sun now arrived much further to the left in the morning, almost against the wall. It's been nine weeks since the sun first lit his face that first morning. That meant he missed Thanksgiving. Even with all his work and long hours, he never missed a Thanksgiving dinner with his family. And not just his immediate family of three kids, but they would make the effort for his sister, and her family, and his mother and father, and Yvonne's mother. It was an exciting full house of chaos, and much jocularity.

But not this Thanksgiving. He wasn't there. He wondered how they were taking his missing. Were they still pestering the police? Or had they given him up as dead? The depression weight returned on mass.

I'm really getting sick of bread and peanut butter, he groaned. *I'd give anything for a turkey feast. No, ham. No, Lobster, hmm, buttery lobster. I'm so dry I can't even salivate at the thought.*

The floor was strewn with the water jugs, and jars. Mostly he just kicked them beyond the walking area. The mice had all gone since the rats had arrived. Too bad, they were kinda cute, he thought. Some were even getting friendly. His only friends.

Guess mice don't like rats, he figured.

The rats were in a constant battle with each other to get what they could from the jars, but he left almost nothing. It was actually comical watching them fight over one of the jars. They were his only entertainment. Not quite the live theatre he was used to going to. Oh, look, one was even trying to take a jar under the door. Ah, no. That was funny. First time he'd had a small smile since been in this hell.

When he got up, the rats would scurry away, at first that is. After a few days they just looked at him with a grin of "what the fuck are you going to do about us?"

He lay in the bed and watched as a spider walked upside down along the beam above. Then coming down the dividing wall to the shitter, and towards his feet. Normally he just killed spiders. Disgusting creatures, he cringed.

Itsy, bitsy spider, climbed up the water spout. Down came the rain and washed the spider out. Bitsy spider went up the spout ... again. Bitsy spider. Down the spout. Bitsy spider... Now I can't get that rhyme out of my head, he thought. *Hmm, dee, hum dee...* "Spout...nasty spiders. Fuck me..."

It disappeared around the corner away from him. He was too tired to get up. So, this is what it must be like in solitary confinement, he thought.

What a torturous life, I can't imagine years like this.

He often thought capital punishment was a proper response to some crimes, but now he realized this life was worse than death.

At least they get TV to pass the day. He had nothing but memories. He couldn't even turn that off. This being all-alone was horrible.

I've never felt so depressed.

I just finished a wonderful steak and potatoes dinner with several people from a number of different companies. The yearly convention, this time in San Francisco. Lots of laughing at stupid jokes.

That young woman, just a few seats away from me. Wow, she's got big tits and a low cut dress. Nice cleavage. She is eyeing me. Maybe I'll get lucky.

We dance to the live band, and got tipsy with wine. We strip our clothes off and are having wild sex on the dance floor. She's fondling my face with her fingers.

"What the fuck!" He jumped to his feet. It was black, he couldn't see a thing, but it was clear what was on his face. A rat!

"Fuck! Shit, crap. It could have gnawed my nose off!"

Cautiously he went back to bed. Being so weak, he quickly drifted off in spite of being scared of another rat on him.

Nine weeks. That's how many water jugs were on the floor. Having the straws in fives was a mistake. He should have started them in sevens. He'd know when the next food drop was coming, he thought.

Now I'm so weak I can't even remember if I missed a day. I can't even add up my straws properly.

He tried to rearrange them into sevens, but many fell on the floor and he lost count. So he gave up.

"Life has given up on me," he lamented. *I just sit here on the edge of the bed. That's all I do all day now.*

It was getting cold. But he slept a lot.

He kept having the same dreams over and over. He tried to direct dreams before he slept, something uplifting, something that made him a hero, or a champion, or even a villain, or to get even with his captors. But he just kept dreaming about his former life. Seems like it was someone else's now. Not his own previous existence.

"I feel like shit," he complained.

He hadn't bothered to wash in weeks. Nor his teeth, which meant his gums hurt, and occasionally bled. His mangy knotted hair was long, accompanied by a thick beard.

"Fuck I hate beards," he moaned. "Too itchy."

His bones had been aching for weeks, days at least. He couldn't remember when it started. He hit his right knee on the edge of the bed three days ago, and now he had a huge bruise.

I've never bruised like that before.

He didn't even bother to cut toenails as it hurt too much to bend down, or bring his feet up. Their nails were getting quite long, and curved, with spots of white. He still must be chewing his fingernails. They were all bitten right back.

Don't even know I'm doing it now, I'm so bored.

He spent all day just sitting at the edge of the bed, thinking of a former life, which was fading with each passing day. His only companion was hunger, and the rats of course. They aren't like the mice at all, he realized.

He'd noticed at least three types of mice. Some with little ears, some with big ears. They don't like each other. Sometimes they scurried chasing each other over his feet. He just sat and watched the theatre actors perform. That was before the rats.

Now all he had were these rats, which seemed to increase in numbers. Little ones, obviously newborns, darted and weaved to get away from the adults who would muscle their way to any food.

"I'm sure they're just waiting for me to die," he lamented. *I'll be nothing but bones picked clean on a rat buffet.* "Christ!"

He was dry all the time now, even after drinking water. His eyes were dry, and sunken, darkness surrounded them like a racoon. He tried to cry a few times when he got overcome with depression, but no tears would form.

"Seems I can't get enough water, yet I've rationed it for a week," he worried.

Funny how the mind works, even in this depth, he thought about sex, often. But now when he did, he didn't get a hard-on. It's been weeks, at least. He forgot when the last one was.

"Too damned weak to jerk off anyway,' he whimpered. *God, I miss sex. I miss tits in my face. Someone riding me.* "Goddammit, I gotta stop thinking about this. Look, nothing is happening anyway, it just lays there limp."

"I'm going to die here. What's taking so long?"

Rained again today. Busy day too. Something to do, a challenge. He managed to fill one water jug completely. Cloudy stinking water. At least he could wash now. His spirits heightened. He could even use the water to wash his pants, he realized. Took days for them to dry. No one to see him naked anyway, he thought. The rash between his balls was worse now, plus big pusy pimples on his ass too.

I haven't had those since being a teenager.

It got colder. He could see his breath.

How many straws? I can hardly see.

The wall was fuzzy. He ended up just putting in a new set of straws after a food drop. "One, two, three, four, five... five.... What the fuck comes after five? Oh, right, six. Six straws. He should get a food drop tomorrow night. Eight fucking weeks. No, ten weeks. Ten. There are ten water jugs on the floor."

Time didn't exist, there was no relative change in time except the coming darkness of each cycle. Day light was shorter too, he found himself enveloped in black before he was ready to sleep. He sat at the edge of the bed in the dim, listening to the rats scurrying around.

It was a struggle to get out of bed when light did return. It was raining again.

Fucking water dripping on me, so what.

The rash on his neck from the collar was bleeding, had been on and off for days. Some green thick pus was on his hand from it – it smelled bad, rotted meat like.

He was sitting at the edge of the bed one morning, chewing on a bit of bread—the last of it. There was mold on it. The rats won't eat the moldy bread. That's been happening a lot with the cooler temps and the dampness. More mold.

Oh, that fucking dampness. It kept him up at night.

No dreams when I can't sleep.

More rats had been eating his food at night too, he was below his rations because of it. He tried during the day to stop them, but they would just wait for night. He couldn't stop them. He even had some of the bread beside him on the bed to protect it. But he woke up with a rat on his chest eating the bread. Ballsy rodents.

They even ate the dried puke from all those days back. He was so desperate, he thought about eating it himself a couple times.

"If I could only catch one these rats, I'd eat it raw," he growled.

Every day was spent sitting doing nothing but watch them. Sometimes they would fuck right in front. "Do rats have orgasms," he wondered. *I miss orgasms. I've lost all emotions now. I don't fucking care any more. Just get this over with, please.*

Week twelve. Maybe. He managed to count twelve water jugs, though it took more than one try. He didn't bother with the straws any more. Food came when it came.

It was real cold now. Near freezing. Not there yet. Water on the floor wasn't freezing. But it will.

I'll be here to see it freeze.

It snowed during the night. The window was buried in it this morning. The room was dark, almost no light could get in, but a faint glow through the snow.

"Now no more sun will come in my window," he thought. It was the only joy in the morning. A light of hope. Gone, so was his hope, he groaned.

By mid day the snow melted, and light returned.

In the waning light he watched two rats fucking on the floor. They had just stopped, and scurried away. They've never done that before. A clicking sound echoed. The doorknob turned and the door opened.

A bright light burst through the black, hurting his eyes. A flashlight! Someone's there!

Is it possible I've been rescued?

"So, you're still alive are you," a voice said. A familiar voice. He knew that voice.

Have I been rescued? I've been rescued! Life will get back to normal!

His body filled with energy.

"Thank God you found me. Praise the Lord you rescued me!"

"No," the voice said.

His heart sunk, he stopped in mid emotion. It was the kidnapper.

"Did you get paid you fucker!?"

"No. I'm not asking for any money."

"Then what the fuck am I doing here? Who are you?"

"Your saviour."

"My what? My saviour? What the fuck are you talking about?"

"I've come to give you the chance to make peace with yourself."

"Who the fuck are you?" He stood up with all the might he could, and walked as far as the chain would let him. He could see clearer. The end of double-barrelled shotgun was pointing right at him. The flashlight was attached to the barrel. Part of the beam reflected off the top of the blue metal. But he couldn't see who it was. The light was kept on the man's face.

"Put the fucking light down and let me see your face."

"Keep guessing," he says. "Who do you think wants you dead?"

"No one, why would anyone want me dead? I've done nothing wrong."

"Nothing wrong!? Well, that really doesn't surprise me. You never did think you did anything wrong."

"WHO ARE YOU?"

"I told you. But I'll give you a hint. Remember the lawsuit against you?"

"Yeah, how do you… Oh, fuck. It's YOU! You put me in this hellhole? Do you even know how much I have suffered in here, for wha—"

"YOU suffered? I've been suffering for ten years because of you! Cock, mother fucking prick!"

The man was confused. "How have you suffered? You got money from me. You took MY money!"

"You have no clue, do you? You never did. You emotionally

react to situations, you never think before you act. Your actions have impacted how many people? How many people like me have you destroyed? No more. You're done destroying."

"We settled this. Now you want even more from me? You signed an agreement to never come near me again. You will go to jail for this!"

"I think not."

"You want more money, well forget it. You get fuck all from me."

"I already got your money."

"You got piddley little from me, not even a year's pay worth."

"Two years, Shithead. Two years not, one, and that was just the beginning."

"You…, no more money, you signed an agreement. What do you want?"

"A confession."

"A what? You're fuckn' CRAZY!"

"It's a free country, I have every right to be crazy."

Now the man's blood was boiling. New energy of rage filled him. He was getting fight back in him. "Arg!! You are just mind fucking me!"

"Have you gone crazy yet?"

"Of course, anyone chained like mangy dog to a wall would go crazy! Christ!"

"Good, then I have achieved my task, almost…"

Achieved his task? Making me suffer is achieving his task? He's making me suffer because I fired his ass ten years ago? Does this guy not get over anything? Almost? What does he mean by almost? There is more to come?

"…just one thing left. Your life has been one of control. You try to control everyone you come in contact with…"

"Of course, that's how I built by business, so what?" the man interjected.

"…no one has been able to control you. Except for my lawsuit. You were totally helpless, and out of control. It was wonderful to see you flapping like a fish out of water. But it wasn't enough. You didn't learn. So here you are. In a place where you have no control at all. Nothing. Not what you eat, nothin'.

"So, I'm going to force you to get control over one last thing. You're going to make a choice. You're going to confess that you're an evil person. You use people and throw them away like dirt. You confess that your entire life has been a disgrace and a waste and I will fire both barrels into you right now and put you out of your misery. If you don't, I have a bag of food here, enough for three weeks, and a blanket and some new clothes. It'll have to do you until it runs out. Then you starve.

"Maybe you'll be rescued, maybe you won't. I know you like to take risks, that's how you've gotten ahead. But for once in your life you're going to make a choice on *your* life, not others. This is the only chance of getting any control back, about living and hoping, or dying right now."

That was funny, the man laughed at him. First time he'd laughed since being here. This guy was a nut case.

I fired his ass for screwing up an account. He took retribution on me, even won his case. Now he wants me to choose my own death? His way? Fuck him.

"Fuck off," the man said sitting down

"So you don't think you did anything wrong."

"I'm not talking to you. You'll be caught. Now get out."

"Suit yourself. I'm going to give you a week to think about this. I'll come back and ask you to choose again."

More food was put on the table, and a couple blankets were tossed over the food. A cooler with a lid that closes to keep the rats away, was slid along the floor from out of the darkness.

Before the door was closed came the voice, "Oh, and by the way, you gave me a great Christmas present. I got the money you stashed in the Caribbean."

The light went out, the door closed, and it clicked locking the man in the prison again.

What? He got my stash? No way, no one knows about my stash. Not even my wife. It's my rainy day money. How could he possibly know let alone get the money. He's bluffing. Or is he? He knows about it? No, he's guessing. He's mind fucking with me. He knows nothing about my stash.

But the thought occurred to him; *I'm going to die alone.* Rage was trumped by that panic feeling again. It was the worse panic attack ever.

He screamed, "I'll find you! I'll kill you! You won't get away with this!"

He threw the food around the room screaming. He kicked the cooler to the far wall, hurting his toes in the process, which just enraged him even more. Worse, he threw the blankets across the room beyond his reach. Wonderful.

PART 2

My Investigation

Day 1, Monday Sept 13th

I was just about to pay for my coffee at the McD's drive through on North Western when my Samsung blasted the Dragnet theme.

I stumbled to get the dollar-fifty from the tray in the centre consol, while my phone kept demanding I answer.

"Hello," I said with one hand putting the coffee in the cup holder.

"Marg, when are you getting here?"

"Hi David, nice you say good morning first. I'm just down the road getting my coffee fix. Why, what's up?"

"Got another for your plate."

I collapsed the phone mid message. Swell. Just what I needed, another case file. I'm going twenty-four seven now as it is. Damn budget cuts. I don't care if Chicago is bankrupt; criminals are having a field day with continued downsizing of police.

The Fourteenth District Station was only five minutes away.

I walked into Captain David Doroszuk, office. Actually, he was called Chief David, long before I knew him. Apparently, the story goes he was, on his mother's side, a descendant of Mohawks, or Mohicans, or something. So he was part Native American, to be politically correct. Something about that hooked nose gave him away.

As usual he was his prickly self. Balding, and over weight, a far cry from his former US Marine drill sergeant days thirty years ago. A complete by-the-book cop.

He'd had his years in the police field. If anyone knew criminals, it was Doroszuk. God knows he'd put a lot of them away, even mobster murderers. If Doroszuk couldn't get them on murder, he would figure out fraud that would stick. Some say the Mob had a price on his head. Some say he also slept with a 1911 45cal pistol loaded and cocked under his pillow.

Taking off his reading glasses, he handed me a folder with a big smile on his face. When he smiled at you you knew you're screwed.

"Why me? There's others who can take a new one."

"No, you have the fewest cases," he said sitting back down behind his desk.

"Like fuck I do."

"I've made my decision on the size of each case. You have to take this one." He was smiles from ear to ear as he leaned back into his chair.

"Swell. What's this shit?"

"It'll be a quickie. Some executive, Nick Easton. He's missing. His wife called Saturday. Two uniforms interviewed her last night," he said as he fumbled through some paper. "You have to be at her place by ten am."

"Swell," I said leaving his office.

Another case. Since I've been transferred from vice and promoted to detective of missing persons I've had case after case handed to me. I got promoted early because of the increase in caseload. Mostly stupid small stuff, such as a husband who gets tanked up with friends and doesn't come home. We find him plastered asleep in his car at the side of the road. Such as last night.

Occasionally the missing person is dead, and passed on to homicide if suspected as such. Pretty boring stuff for me mostly. If I'm really good, if I can get a good break, I could get into homicide.

I dreamed of investigating murders since my first days from the academy.

But I'm not there yet. Murder cases are much harder to solve. They can be more complicated than any other type of crime.

One of my last missing persons case was actually fraud, out of state fraud, so the FBI stole from me. I could have solved it too. I was so close.

So now I have another boring case of some executive who didn't come home last night. In a lot of these types of situations they come home later in the day, or sometimes we find out they've been with a prostitute. I had just closed a case like that three days ago when that "missing" person was found down town in a motel with a hooker. Bet the wife sued for divorce.

I was back up to a dozen cases at various stages. It's like juggling. I have to time slice each case. Because of this I have no life. No boyfriend, hell, last time I was proposed to was in grade six by Billy Biss. Soon as someone finds out I'm a cop, and have little time in my life, they don't stay around long. Forty-four and single.

But I wasn't alone. I had a nineteen-year-old daughter, Pamela, and quite the handful. Her father and I had a one-night stand, another cop, from another state no less. Some convention I was at. Stupid, stupid mistake. I thought I had the chance at a life with him, but he wasn't interested at all. He got married several years after our affair.

But we did make a child together. He knows now, after she tracked him down a few years ago when I told her the truth. She spends some summers with him and his family.

And, of course, I have a job partner, Derik Revoy. He's been a cop for twelve years. He came from vice a few months ago. People working vice burn out quickly. He mostly does deskwork now. Some angry pimp put a bullet though Derik's butt. He didn't survive Derik's return fire. But the injury permanently put Derik behind a desk. He does my background research. I go into the field, mostly.

I hated vice, all aspects of it, not just prostitution. There's no satisfaction, no resolution of cases. You're just intruding into people's lives over sex between consenting adults.

I even had to pose undercover as a prostitute once. Didn't work though, Johns knew right away I was a cop. Guess I couldn't get the lingo down right, or something. Besides, there was so much murder and fraud taking place that vice had been deemed less of a priority. Lots of cops had been rotated off vice, I was one of them.

Derik was great with finding stuff out, a real waste in vice. His injury was my gain. He came from a huge family, on both sides of his parents. He had more cousins than I had friends, but then again, I had few friends. I went to one of his family events on Labour Day. It was packed. How the hell he remembered all their names was beyond me.

The great part of all that extended family was they worked in various city departments. Most were cops, some in various clerk's offices, one, his sister, was a city councillor. Thus, when he needed to find out something, his cousins would put him to the top of the list. We'd get great turn around time.

The best part of Derik was he remembered my coffees. If he wasn't married, I'd have my eye on him even though he was a few years younger than me.

Dragnet played again. "Marg, are you coming back to the office?" Derik asked.

"No point, my meeting with Easton's wife is in thirty minutes. Hinsdale is just about that far from here."

"We got a call from the hospital. I'm sorry, Marg, but your mom's had a stroke. They took her to Mercy."

Mom… Oh shit. My heart sunk.

"Marg, you there?"

"Yeah… Thanks Derik. Can you cancel my meeting with Easton? Make it for tomorrow instead."

"Sure, absolutely. I'm sorry, Marg, I pray to God it's not bad."

I turned around, and headed to Mercy Hospital.

I hated hospitals. I hated seeing people in hospitals. It's people at their most vulnerable, and it exposes so clearly that we are mortal. My last experience was not good. My father died right in front of me. Took days, but I couldn't leave his side. Tubes came out of every orifice, and some new ones. He couldn't talk at all. It was so undignified. He definitely wouldn't have liked it. He was homicide Chief of D's at the end, 40 years as a cop. It took its toll on him.

They just turned off the ventilation machine, and in thirty minutes he was no more. Gone. Cancer.

Mom had been fairly well, in spite of being 72, or so she told me last week. Yes, I was late in their lives, and their only child.

On her last visit to her doctor she had high blood pressure, sure, but who didn't in those days in that hell of an economy. The doctor wasn't overly concerned. So what precipitated this attack?

I came up to the ward nervous and very concerned. Was she out of it? I was thinking the worse, who doesn't.

As I came through the door, she was awake and upright.

"Hey, Marg," she said in a bit of a slur. Something was definitely different. The left side of her face looked limp, she wasn't moving her left arm. She just raised her right hand opposite to me.

"Hi mom, what happened?"

"I'm not sure, one minute I was in the bathroom, having a bowel movement, the next I'm here."

Thank you, MediAlert. She was opposed to it at first, of course. Clearly the best dollars I've ever spent.

"Has the doctor seen you yet?"

"Yes, couple hours ago. He said I had a stroke on my right side. I can't move my left leg nor my left arm."

That was the end of her independence. She wasn't going to be able to live in her home. And she definitely wouldn't be able to come and live in my apartment. I had no time to look after her.

"It's OK Margery, I'm not coming to live with you."

She read my mind.

"I'm going to sell the house and everything. I've been planning this for a while, since your father passed. I've already signed up at a home. A while back I did just in case this happened, you know. Sorry, but there won't be any inheritance left for you, I'm afraid dear."

So much for Dad's double and triple shifts for forty years. He didn't live to enjoy that money, now the rest had to look after my Mom. I had to think about her quality of life. Better at a home for sure.

"But it's not in Chicago, Margery, dear. It's outside Madison. You know, the one your aunt May is in. It will be better for the both of us, dear."

"But that's going to be more difficult for me to come see you. Maybe once a week at best. My work load is over-powering."

"That's OK, dear, I know you have your job. That's more important than an old cripple like me."

"Don't talk like that, Mom!"

"It's true. All my friends are dead. Your daughter rarely comes to see me any more…" That was a lie, Pam loved her Gran, even though she had a busy life. With me working while Pam was growing up, my parents had to raise her. For that I was eternally grateful. So Pam did pay regular visits. "…so I might as well go be with my sister. We can die together there."

She was getting depressed and melodramatic again. Ever since Dad died it had gotten worse. I'd wondered how Dad put up with her when it got real bad. But he did, brave and loyal man he was to tolerate her periodic depression bouts. I remembered it being so bad she would lash out at him with real nasty insults. He would come to my place in tears. But he'd always understood it was the depression talking and he would go home within hours.

Mom hadn't had that shoulder to take out her frustrations on for nearly five years now. So, I'd been the brunt of some of her depression bouts. In a way, going that far away to a home was a blessing to some degree.

Twenty minutes was all I could take. I just couldn't stand there helplessly looking at her in that state. My job depended on me not getting distracted. But I needed to contact Pamela. I didn't look forward to telling her this.

I scrolled my short list, and hesitantly hit her record.

"Hello?"

"Pam, it's your mother. Your grandma had a stroke. She's in

Mercy. Hos—"

"What? I'm coming right away…"

A dial tone remained. With Mom raising Pam, they were very close, unlike between us. So, this would definitely be crushing to her.

Dragnet took me from my thoughts.

"Marg, it's Derik. I've rescheduled your meeting with Mrs. Easton for 2:00PM. Couldn't get anything tomorrow."

"Ok, that'll work, thanks." There I was, back to the real world.

North Clay Street in Hinsdale was one of those expensive exclusive residences. Million dollar homes, many of which had For Sale signs on them. More than a few had "REDUCED" patched over the sign. A common indication of the state of the economy.

Easton's drive was cobblestone ending in a two-car garage on the left of the house. The home was two story of brick and stone. Definitely more than a million dollars. The landscaping was impeccable, nothing out of place. People in these homes paid to have their lots manicured. Easton did well indeed.

The door was answered by the maid, a young Latino woman, appropriately dressed in the part. I waited in the foyer for Mrs. Easton. The house was perfect. Nothing was out of place. The living room to the right looked like no one had ever been in it, a showcase. A glass cabinet had golf and skiing trophies, with photos of Easton, I presumed, holding those trophies.

Same with the dinning room on the left. It was laid out with an oak dinning set, obviously very expensive. Luxurious paintings were on the walls.

The hardwood floors were glowing from the refection off the massive chandelier in the entrance hall, not a scuffmark anywhere.

And Easton had kids? No way a house looked like that with young children. There wasn't a toy anywhere in sight, not even outside.

The maid told me to take my shoes off. No shoes allowed in the house.

Easton's wife, Yvonne, came down the wide stairs on the wall on the living room side. She was wearing a dress ready for company.

She was ordained with lots of jewellery. Rocks the size of peanuts were on her fingers, different colours as well as clear. She looked a woman pushing up against forty trying to look twenty. Her blond hair was definitely coloured. Her face was tight, like plastic (too much Botox I thought), a flat stomach —no one that age, popping out kids, had a flat stomach unless manicured like their property. And those breasts. No one near forty had perky breasts like that. Those were stuffed.

The perfect wife to fit the perfect museum house.

As she got to the bottom she ordered the maid to make tea and prepare the kitchen. In a stern voice, she reminded the maid to go and pick up the kids after school. She barely noticed me. No introduction at all. The maid had to invite me down the hall towards the kitchen behind Yvonne.

"Any news on my husband?" Yvonne said matter of factually.

I sat down at the small table between the kitchen and family room. A large flat screen filled the far wall over a stone fireplace. The family room was sunken down below the rest of the first floor grade. Though there were a few toys, neatly placed on shelving against the right wall, the room was, like the rest of the house, immaculate. Nothing was out of place.

But what was out of place where any pictures. Not one family photo was on a wall, anywhere. If I didn't know first hand the Easton's had children, you wouldn't have guessed it from the pristine condition of the house, and lack of any family photos. The fridge didn't have any kid's magnetic alphabets on it. Everyone who has kids has alphabets on their fridges!

"We haven't found him yet," I said getting my pad and pen out.

"You're new. Why are you a new person on this file?" she said sitting across from me.

What did she mean by new? That I was too young? "I was next in line to get your case," I said.

She huffed. She was very defensive looking, and starting to shuffle in her chair. There was something going on here. She continued.

"My husband runs a perfectly legitimate company. If he has gone missing there must be foul play going on."

"What do you mean by foul play?" I ask taking notes, not just of what she says, but how she says it.

"As you can see we are rich," she said with her nose firmly in the sky. "He's been kidnapped."

"We don't jump to conclusions." I doubted they were rich enough to get kidnapped for ransom.

"Well, why else would he been gone? Maybe he's dead somewhere along the road. He may be a victim of a car jacking. He has an expensive car you know. Found it yet?"

"Mrs. Easton, we don't speculate. We gather evidence…"

"How may cops do you have looking for my husband?" she demanded.

"Enough. I'd like to ask a series of questions, if I may."

She didn't look too comfortable, and barked a command to the maid to leave the kitchen. The first impression I got was that this maid was a slave. I was sure she got paid as little as possible, and worked as much as possible, twenty-four-seven.

"Yes, ma'am. I'll clean the bathroom," the maid said and left for up stairs.

Yvonne looked at her watch. "Pick up the kids in twenty minutes," she commanded. She then stared blankly at me.

"Mrs. Easton, please understand these questions are purely routine. I have to ask them," I said.

"Fine," she said folding her arms, a bit of pout on her face.

"How often does your husband leave like this?"

"Never," she said looking out the window, not at me.

Never. Right, lie number one.

"His business takes him on trips, is that correct?"

"Yes, but he has no trips planned." She was still looking, blankly, out the window. She was uncomfortable answering questions.

"When was the last time you heard from him?"

"Two days ago, at around six. He called to say he was going to be late for dinner. He never came home. Look, I already answered these questions to the two cops who came here. Why are you asking them again?"

"I need to." Of course I did, not for the answers, I had the cop's notes with me, it was her I wanted to judge, not her answers. Of course, we always have to make sure answers match to the same questions asked at different times by different cops. "May I continue, please?"

She huffed and looked out the window.

"Does he do that a lot?"

"Do what a lot?"

Ok, this is being evasive. "Is he late for dinner a lot?"

"Of course, he has a business to run." That response made her look at me, as if I was the stupid one.

"What time does he usually show up home?"

"Depends. Sometimes after midnight."

"Any times he doesn't come home?"

"Sometimes, he will call if that happens." She was fidgeting again in the seat, adjusting her dress.

"Does your husband go out on the town with any friends? Stay out late from those events?"

"Sometimes, but again, he will call me."

"And no call after six pm."

"That's what I said," with that stern look at me again.

Different sort of questions now. "How's your marriage?"

Now that made her perk right up. "Marriage? What does my marriage to Nick have to do with him missing?" She started to play with the rings on her fingers.

"Just routine. Covering all bases, ma'am."

"That's intrusive. I don't like it." She resumed looking out the window, still twirling a ring.

"Please answer the question."

"We're a perfect couple. Nick loves me very much. There is no one in Nick's life but me. Can't you see that with all this?" she said displaying the rocks on her fingers.

Liar and show off.

"Have you found Nick's car?" she asked again.

"No, we haven't."

"Where ever his car is you should find Nick. He loves his car… But not more than me."

That was an after thought.

"We've no hits on the whereabouts of your husband's car." Actually, I hadn't had time to initiate that yet. "I've got few more questions, if I may please."

"Fine," she said and resumed looking out the window.

"Does your husband have any enemies?"

She turned and looked at me with a WTF expression.

"Enemies? What do you mean? No one hates Nick." She finished with that same 'are you stupid or something' look.

"Everyone has enemies, ma'am."

"Not Nick, he's a perfect gentleman."

Another lie, no man is a 'prefect gentleman.' This was going nowhere. I wasn't going to get an honest answer from this woman.

"OK, I think we're done here, I want to thank you for the tea." I hadn't drunk any. "That's it? You're leaving now?" She was getting anxious. "I demand to know what you are going to do to find my husband!"

"Ma'am, we are putting all the resources we can to find him." That was just me, and Derik of course. "I'm going to check the morgue…"

"The morgue!!??" she screeched.

Oh, she did not like that. Though, I wondered if she was more concerned with her continued lifestyle.

"Yes, that's routine. I'll check the hospitals too. Then I'll check with people at your husband's office see if anyone there knows anything. I'll also need your husband's cell phone number. We should be able to track him with that."

I wrote it down, got up and headed to the door. Yvonne followed me, as if I had broken some protocol. She called for the maid to get the door for me.

"That's OK, I can see myself out," I said. No use, by that time I gotten my shoes back on. The maid had flown down the stairs and held the door open for me.

The only thing Yvonne said as I walked out the door was, "Find my husband!" Not even a please. Hell, she never said please to the maid either. Stuck up bitch.

Soon as I got into the car I called Easton's cell. I only got his message service. I called Derik to put a trace on it.

Day 2, Tuesday Sept 14th

First thing I did when I got in was to initiate a search for Easton's car. I got the VIN off the dealer he bought it from. The car was barely a year old, a 2014 Mercedes-Benz SL65 AMG. I got Derik to find the car's location through its built in GPS.

Derik came in and placed a java beside me. But I had already started to suck on one. "I'd swear you're trying to drug me."

"So, how did it go yesterday?" he said taking a drink from the cup he offered me.

"She's more worried about losing her lifestyle, I think. Just sent a notice to look for his car."

"This is day three isn't it?" Derik asked.

"Yep, so we can count out being drunk somewhere, or out with a hooker. I need to see his workers. Can you set that up? I have a court date this afternoon, so I gotta get this paper work done."

"Sure. Hey, did you hear? The garbage union voted to strike. Midnight tonight. We're going to have one stinking city now."

Didn't city workers realize Chicago was twelve billion in under funded pension liabilities? Yes, they did, they just didn't care the city finances were a mess. It didn't matter to them that the city was broke.

Things were so bad, even overtime for us was halted. There's no way the garbage union was going to get any raises. In fact, the mayor threatened to cut their salaries, which was what prompted the strike.

The courthouse was packed, like it's been for years. I worked on this case a long time. Three years ago. It was my last vice case. Some rich businessman was caught smuggling booze up to Canada. I stumbled upon his stash by accident investigating him for not having a licence for his illegal bar. He was making the booze in his basement and selling it.

We nailed him on that last year, but this day was his court date for the trafficking across the boarder.

Waiting I had time to think about Easton's case. The wife really bothered me. I'd seen such people before, real bitches. I wouldn't surprise me Easton had left her. But I had to stay objective.

My case was called. I gave my testimony. Then it all stopped. His lawyer interrupted and claimed that without a search warrant specific for the exporting of the booze, the case should be dismissed.

The judge called the two lawyers to the bench. I was worried. I'd seen this scumbag lawyer before. He was called the magician because he could always pull a rabbit out of his hat. I had a sinking feeling the case was going to be dismissed.

Sure enough, the lawyers went back to their seats, and the judge ruled my search of his car was not part of the warrant to search his premises looking for his moonshine. The case was dismissed.

I was pissed. So much work for nothing. What a waste of my day.

Day 3, Wednesday Sept 15th

I got the call first thing in the morning that the hospital was discharging my mom. I had to pick her up and take her to the nursing home.

I was pissed they would throw her out so fast having a stroke. I argued with the lady on the phone, but they were adamant. She had to leave today, she was stable enough to be moved.

Such is the state of our healthcare system.

I don't like Madison much. I'm more comfortable in my own city. We swung by my mom's home, but she didn't want to bring much. The house was going up for sale. I had just gotten off the phone with an agent. He wasn't too hopeful.

Home prices had been falling, the price he thought we might get, maybe a year from now, wouldn't cover my mother's residence payments. Between my mother's bank account, and the few stocks from my father she had left that I knew of, she might be able to last a few years.

If the house didn't sell, or not sell for enough, I would have no choice but to pony up the difference to keep my mom there. Not what I was looking forward to.

The nursing home was a nice place, but nice places cost. Her reunion with my aunt was a joy to watch. They loved each other deeply. My mom was going to be just fine here.

I came back to a roadblock in the downtown near the precinct. Another near riot was in Chicago today. The Occupy Movement, again, demanding money for the poor. Where do these people think the money will come from? They called some of my squad to help out with the quelling of the rioters. Luckily, I got the day off to move mom.

It's times like that I boiled about the United States. We used to be so full of wealth. But today, we were so poor and getting poorer. I'm not a political person, my focus was the law, keeping the peace and helping people. But times like this makes one think one should have been more acute to what was happing.

Derik called. He couldn't get the company to agree to an interview with all the staff until the 16th, tomorrow. Seemed with their boss gone, they were like a chicken with its head cut off. Meetings were missed, clients were getting angry, deadlines would be missed, mistakes were already happening. And this was just the first few days of his absence.

Still no hit on Easton's car. I turned at the next available free side street, dodged traffic, and headed home.

During the drive I wondered why Easton's company would want to waste another day for me to interview them regardless of their chaos.

That night mom called. She needed more from the house. I would have to make another trek to Madison in the morning. With fuel at being over five dollars per gallon, it was going to get expensive real fast.

Day 4, Thursday Sept 16th

There we were at Insur-Data and it took a lot of pressure to get the father to agree for the both of us to interview everyone, one at a time. Easton's father, Macalister, was the company CFO. He was a retired investment bank executive. According to Derik, he'd been trying to make up for the loss of his son. He was our point man in the company, not the second in command. He told us who could be interviewed and when, and for how long. Only ten minutes each. He claimed he couldn't lose much time from their work.

Derik interviewed the staff, all women, the significance of which I would find out later.

I interviewed the second in command first, George Finley, then Macalister.

Finley didn't have anything. The last he saw of Easton, around 8 pm, was two hours before Easton was to leave the office the night of his disappearance. They were working on a crucial file for a meeting the next day. He said there was no way Easton would miss a meeting worth several hundred thousand dollars.

The father didn't have much. He was also working on the same file, leaving around the same time as Finley. Easton's father was, obviously, very distraught.

"He told me he was heading home around 10pm, no later. Do you think my son's been... you know, killed? Murdered perhaps?"

"Mr. Easton, we don't speculate at this point. I would not think that this early in the investigation."

"It's not like him to do this. I've been calling his cell all day, nothing. His voice mail is full. He's very prompt at getting back to people. This isn't like him. Not at all. This isn't like him. Something's wrong, something's very very wrong."

He paused to get some composure.

"It's possible," I said, "But, we've got no evidence of anything wrong, Mr. Easton. Unless you know someone who would want to do your son harm."

He looked at me with tears. He thought a bit. "No. No, I don't know anyone who would want to do Nicky harm."

"He had no threats against him? No hints he was in trouble?"

"No, not that I... oh, wait. We've had some threats. We've had to lay a few people off recently, you understand. You may want to check some of our past employees."

"You have reason to suspect previous employees?"

"I'll leave that for you to do. Do your job. I'll make sure you get the list of all employees we've had."

"Did you keep these threats? E-mails, letters perhaps?"

"No, just phone calls."

"Do you know who made the calls?"

"No, I'm sorry, they didn't leave a forwarding number. Now that I think about this more. That must be it. Someone we used to have here has killed my son."

"Mr. Easton, please don't jump to any conclusions. We go on the evidence, not gut feelings."

Mr. Easton took me to where his son parked his car. It was at the side of the building. I looked around the pavement, then around the grass to the road. Nothing. I walked out to the middle of the road to take in the scene.

The building Insur-Data was in was a former small factory. Insur-Data rented the top office floors. The lower level, the old factory floor, was partitioned off for four other companies.

The road was a short cul-de-sac with some dozen similar factories of various sizes. To the west was the main thoroughfare. To the east, one more factory over from Insur-Data, was the loop of the cul-de-sac. A train was slowly passing by beyond that.

The next factory to the west was abandoned and being torn down. It was entirely fenced off.

I walked to the fence separating the railway line from the loop in the road. There were a number of railway cars in one factory siding to the north, just the rail line to the south with factories butting up to the tracks. Beyond the tracks was a block concrete wall with a large factory beyond that. The noise from which was loud.

There was a fare amount of bush along the tracks and that wall. The area was littered with garbage, tires, and even an old mattress. A hole was in the fence where people were getting through. If Easton's body was around there, it would had been found.

I walked back to Insur-Data. The east side of the building were the large doors for trucks to load and unload. Down the west side of the building were the fronts of the other companies. The first one occupied about half of the factory floor. They made fibreglass bathtubs and hot tubs. Even in this economy, people were still putting in hot tubs? How could they afford that with such high power bills?

I went inside to talk to the employees. They didn't have a nightshift, and only the storefront was open on Saturdays.

The next unit made kitchen cabinets. It was a father and son business. I talked with one of the sons who was working the night of Easton disappeared. He went for a smoke around 3am that morning.

"Did you see an expensive sports car parked down there?" I asked him pointing towards the road.

"Maybe, I don't remember. I can't really see up there. I know the car you mean. Nice car. It may have been there. Sometimes they do work late up there. I don't know what they do, but sometimes that, and other cars, are there over night."

"So, as far as you know that car was there at 3am?"

"I wouldn't say that. It might have been. I left around 8am and the lot up there was empty. That I remember."

I went to the next company. They wrote animation software for children's shows and commercials. They had three shifts. No one could remember if or when Easton's car was parked there. Many of those employees had expensive cars, so no need to gawk at Easton's.

The last unit of the factory was empty.

I left with a bit of confusion. Did Mr. Easton think some past employee had something to do with his son's disappearance? Stranger things have happened.

Derik got nothing from the other staff, they had all left around 5pm save the three main officers staying for late night workload.

Mom's mood was better, so Aunt May told me. I came at a good time, she was sleeping. It was quiet time like this, with nothing else to think about, that you ponder one's own future, one's own mortality. What I saw in my mom was my own future in thirty years.

I needed to leave. I couldn't be infected with thoughts like that. But mom woke as I started out the door.

"Margery, dear, how nice to see you," she said. The slurring was worse, maybe because she just work up.

We talked for about an hour, but the slurring didn't improve.

I had to cut my visit short. Mom was crying as I left. That's all I needed.

Day 5, Friday Sept 17th

For once the squad room was quiet. Everyone was trying to catch up on paperwork before the weekend. I was preparing for a court appearance that afternoon. In the hallway I could hear that dreaded voice. Don Norman. His nickname was Abby-Normal. Norman = Normal = Abnormal = Abby-Normal, like from the *Young Frankenstein* movie. The name suited him. He was over six foot five, very thin with black hair. I sure hoped he didn't come in here.

Norman was in the same high school as me, but two years ahead. He started on the force in the group after me. Last week he was reassigned to fraud from homicide. The department had to cycle people from homicide to other divisions to give them a break. I sure hoped I got his vacancy in homicide. I just needed to clean my cases from my desk.

The only draw back of going to homicide is I'd have to wear a gun. I didn't have to in missing persons. I don't like to carry guns. Sometimes I had to in vice. Most of the time I just left my Glock in my desk.

Not that I don't like guns, it's the people I have to interview who don't like them. If I needed to intimidate a witness I got Derik to come with me, he was always armed. I found it better to not be armed when dealing with ordinary people. Good cop, bad cop does work.

But Norman, he never stopped talking, and about completely trivial subjects. The previous week he cornered me in the hallway to tell me about the price of steaks at the local food store. Like I gave a shit. But he went on, and on, and on, and... You get the picture. I'm sure you've come across such people. Confronted like this, most people would be courteous; you don't want to just walk away.

If it was a phone call from Norman, some of my squad mates would put the phone down, walk away, and when they got back Abby-Normal would still be talking about the same thing.

Every time I encountered him I always meant to later find out if people like him have some kind of official medical mental disorder that makes them yak, and yak, on and on. But then again, it's likely we all have some kind of "mental disorder."

My escape was usually to look at the time and say I was late for something. I hoped he would just bypass us.

Bloody hell, not that time. He came through the door. I heard it. Some guys got up to retreat from him before he started. That left me holding the bag.

I think my squad mates did that deliberately.

Best not to look up, I thought. It would be an invitation to start one of his meaningless conversations. I had a ton of paperwork to catch up on.

Swell. He pulled another chair over to be beside me on the right. I fucking hate it when people interrupt me.

We had a fifty-two inch flat screen in the lunchroom, which had CNN on all day. I liked to keep up with what's going on in the world, especially the European financial implosion, as the ramifications for us would, and was, profound. Hell, the US Administration was driving this country into the toilet. I wanted to keep up with the on goings of the world.

So when I had my occasional lunch I liked to watch the TV and concentrate on what was being said. Yet people are so ignorant, they must think we aren't watching, just staring at nothing on the screen. I don't know. Norman would have to interrupt and try to start a conversation. And it was always when a key bit of information was being said, and I would miss it.

I think the only time I saw Norman speechless was when we were all glued to the TV during the 9/11 attacks.

I'd have to tell him, politely as I could, that I was trying to listen. That's why I had it on. Guess that made me a snob. I know some of them talk about me behind my back. Fuck 'em.

But now Normal was doing his, well, normal. I needed to concentrate on getting this paper work done. I had to be out in an hour for the court case.

He pulled right up to me and put his arm on the back of my chair.

"How goes it, Marg?" he said.

"Busy Norm." I so much wanted to say "Abby".

"You're always busy. You really need to relax. Why don't the two of us take the afternoon off and take in a movie?"

This was not the first time Abby-Normal tried to ask me out. He was definitely not my type. Abby-Normal had been married three times, recently divorced – again. He fancied himself far too much. Reminded me of the Seinfeld character Elaine dated, the big car salesman. They looked similar too.

But us women have the perfect out. "Norm, if you don't mind moving your arm, I have to go to the washroom."

"Oh sure."

I got up and as I walked out the door he said, "I'll catch you later!"

No, he won't. I went down the stairs to the front door, where Derik was just coming in. "Hey, Derik, Abby-Normal is waiting for you in the squad room. I have appointments. See you later." I run past him out the door. Pay back is so sweet.

I got back later that afternoon for our usual meet with Chief David to brief him on our cases.

I was pleased to announce the court found my guy guilty on all charges of selling porn on line. I was one of several detectives from different local forces. Another case that took years to get through the system. But I was pleased with my work. It nailed his ass. It was a feather in my cap.

"So, how's the Easton case?" Doroszuk asked looking at other paperwork.

"Nothing, no hit on his VIN yet. We interviewed the staff yesterday, not much to go on. But the father, he's their CFO, was a bit evasive when I asked about the company finances. He seems to think someone they fired may have something to with Easton's disappearance. We're checking the list."

"It's a week tomorrow, right, that he's been missing?"

"Correct."

"What do you think?"

"I don't know what to think. I'd expect we'd find his car by now."

"Think he's taken off?"

"If he has I'll find him. He'll leave some kind of trail. We've found nothing on his credit cards. No meals. No gas. Nothing."

"He's using cash," David suggested.

"Assuming he's alive, yes. It could also mean he's dead."

"You know, if you think there's foul play I'll have to send it up stairs."

"Oh, no, you won't. I'm no where near that conclusion."

"One more week, Marg. Then I'll have to send the file to homicide."

Saturday Sept 18th

The visit to Mom was tiring. There is no way I could visit every weekend like this. Traffic on a Saturday was shit. Accidents caused hour-long waits. Was it me, or was the bad economy making people drive worse? I was glad to get home for a few hours of peace and quiet.

I had just seated after my dinner to get into a book lent to me by Derik: *Blinding White Flash*. One of two in the series. It was written by a new author, his first book, but Derik said it was "phenomenal from start to finish". Pam called me before I could even get past the first few pages. She was in a real tizzy.

"Mom, I'm pregnant."

I was speechless. My baby, having her first child. She's not even married, with a crappy job as a cashier at the food store. But I was going to be a grandmother. The thought pleased me. But then I realized. I was going to be a grandmother. The thought made me old. I was now my mother.

"Mom, did you hear me?"

"Yes, I did."

"Mom, I'm scared."

Finally, she was scared. Now she was scared. Little too late.

"I have to ask, who's the father?"

"You have to ask me that?"

Her we go, Pam at her best.

"You just think I'm a slut."

Funny how I did the same thing when I was young and stupid, but when my daughter is in the same boat I was in it's unacceptable. The paradox hit home.

"Of course, stupid question. Are you asking me if you should get an abortion?"

"No, Angel…"

Angel? That's a new one, never heard of him. Angel, my ass.

"…he wants to marry me. But I'm scared. You never married."

"Who's Angel, Pam?"

"He works here at the store, staking shelves…"

Oh, great, a loser job, likely a loser boy, wanting to have a baby with my loser daughter. But then again, his gain is my loss. That might not be so bad.

"…but he's a good man."

"How long have you known him, Pam?" Like that really mattered now.

"Three months."

Three months! She's likely three months along.

If she could only see my face. I was doing a major face-palm. But then again, her father and I didn't even know each other before our night. But then again, I don't want my daughter to make the same mistake I did. It's not a good feeling to get smacked in the face with your own hypocrisy.

Day 6, Monday Sept 20th

Derik came into the squad room, and placed a coffee on my desk, went to his desk across from me and sipped his black-no-sugar. "I got that list of fired employees." He passed the list over to me.

"Fired employees?" I looked confused.

"Insur-Data. It's a complete list of former employees. Remember? You asked me to get the list."

"Right. Anything?"

"Ok, I still don't get it. Why would former employees have anything to do with Easton missing?" Derik said.

"Just being thorough, that's all."

"You're implying someone fired might have killed him?"

"Maybe, never know. Easton's father was concerned about threats to the company by a few of those who were let go."

He shrugged. "Ok. You're the boss."

"Have you been able to contact them all?" I said slurping my java. Ah, the coffee was perfect, just what I needed.

"Not all, about half. Here look at the list." Derik came over to my desk. "There's a pattern here. Big turnover. See, John Greene was the first to get fired, three years after the company started. He was fired not even a year after he was hired. He committed suicide three months later, leaving behind a wife and three small kids."

Now I was starting to get intrigued. Was there a connection between the firing and his suicide? Lots of that was happening with the state of our economy.

"The second one was fired just a couple months later, Bob Rifle.

I talked with him this morning. He replaced Greene. He started his own company putting up fences in Florida. He lost his house, almost lost his wife. He was even hospitalized for a severe nervous breakdown. Easton talked him into joining Insur-Data when he was working for an insurance company, let's see," Derik looked back at the list "Yeah, Ohio State Farm and Auto is the company.

"Rifle was lead project manager for his company. He quit and worked for Easton when the project was done. He blames himself for the stupid judgement. Doesn't blame Easton at all. Just business, Rifle said.

"Then there was Carter Smyth after that," Derik said, handing the paper back to me. "Again fired only a few months after being hired. He's disappeared. No record of being married and his last income tax filing was ten years ago. Either he's dead too, or left the country.

"I have a dozen other people who were hired, and then promptly fired after a few months.

"Ed Whitman was an exception. Whitman was let go ten years after the company started. He was the longest serving employee to get fired. He was easy to find. He used to work for the State as an IT manager before being hired at Insur-Data. In fact, he was the only employee from the beginning. Him and Easton started the company by the looks of it."

"What's that?" I asked. "Whitman was there when the company started?"

"Yep. His retirement from the State started two years *after* the company started, and he has income tax records for both during those years."

"Ok, so let me see if I have this straight. Whitman was there on the first day of the company, left the city, at what age?"

"He worked for the State, not the city. He was forty-seven. He must have retired early."

"…so he took an early retirement then to work for Easton. Then ten years later he's fired?"

"Yep, looks like it."

"So, that means Whitman lost pension money. That must have

pissed Whitman off big time. We have a possible motive here. I want you to pull his financials."

"Why? What's he got to do with Easton's disappearance?"

"Probably nothing, but I hate loose ends. People who lose a lot because of someone hold grudges."

"Well, no judge will give us a warrant to get Whitman's financials. We've nothing to connect him to Easton. Besides, you find out foul play happened here, we lose the case to homicide."

He was right, of course.

Derik went back to his desk. "Ten year old grudges? Ridiculous."

"You know the saying, revenge is a dish best served cold."

Derik looked at me weird, closing his left eye. He does that when he disagrees with me.

"C'mon. You think Whitman has something to do with Easton's disappearance?"

"Stranger things have happened," I said.

Derik threw his hand in my direction dismissing my suggestion. He was probably right.

"Oh, and Derik, did you find where he is?"

"Whitman? Up near Earlville. I tried to call, but no one answered. He has no answering machine either."

Those without answering machines don't want people to contact them.

"So what about the rest of the list, there's several more," Darik said.

"And where are they now?"

"Four are working out of state. One moved to Mexico."

"Thanks. Contact the rest. I want to speak with them all. Now what about Easton's friends, any progress there?"

"Well, seems the father was right. Easton had no friends. I checked. The last one of his old friends to see him was, just a second…" Derik looked at his notes. "Paul Richards. He went to university with Easton, but had lost contact with him when Insur-Data started. So that looks to be a dead end."

"No friends? No golfing buddies?" He did have those trophies. You gotta have friends to boast about your trophies.

"Not that I could find. He only golfed with clients. So that's who he spent his spare time with."

I had other appointments to get to for other cases, so I had to leave.

Ross Turnbull had been missing for three days. He left his car at home, and just vanished. His wife, Virginia, called demanding I come and see some evidence.

It was a total waste of my time. I arrived to an open door of the apartment. Soon as I walked in, the stench was over powering. A torn cat carcass was in the hallway by the door. I had to step over it.

Virginia was on a couch in the living room. Newspapers were all over the place, along with empty dirty dishes. She was sloshed in a bottle. Two empties were on the floor. She owned cats, the only "people" who understand her, she said. They were everywhere.

The place was a total mess. I wasn't surprised her husband left her. Derik found out his bank account was emptied. We were trying to find out if his pension from IBM was sent elsewhere. Likely.

I had no choice that visit. I had to make calls to get her into the hospital, and to get the cats out of the house. Looks like they were so starved they had eaten one of their own.

I thought about my mother after that visit. She didn't have cats, she had fish. Lots of fish tanks. Dad liked the fish too, but when she got so depressed, she didn't want them any more, and Dad had to clean the tanks. Took him all day.

When Dad died, I convinced her to let some of the fish go. I got the thirty gallon tank with Dad's cichlids in it.

This experience with poor Virginia prompted me to call Mom at the home. Bad timing, she was napping. Best I go visit this weekend.

I got home late. Got ready for bed and was looking forward to reading my novel. I had just picked it up and got started. The phone rang. Sigh, I was never going to get to read that book. It was mom. She was in one of the worst bouts of depression I'd seen her in.

"You never want to see me. It's been three days, Margery."

"Mom, I need to work. I have a shit load of cases to solve."

"Your work is always more important than me. I don't want to live any more. I hate this place."

She broke out crying.

"Mom." Nothing but sobbing. "Mom!" I had to say it a dozen times.

"What do you want." It wasn't a question.

"Look, Mom, I'll come up tomorrow morning."

"You're only saying that because I'm crying. You don't care about me."

"No. Mom, I was planning to come this weekend. I'll even take you out shopping."

"Don't bother. You don't mean it."

"Mom, how can I tell you I love you, how I'll be there when you just dismiss me?" I should know by now that trying to be logical to a depressed person is fruitless.

"You don't love me. No one loves me. All my friends are gone. Dead. I don't want to live any more."

"Mom, why are you doing this?"

"I can't help how I feel. All I have to do is die and it will all be over. No more pain. You'd get your inheritance."

"Mom, stop that, please. I don't want your money. Hasn't Pam come to visit this week?"

"No, she doesn't care either. Just like her mother."

"Mom, I care about you."

"Don't bother since it's too much trouble for you."

The conversation went on like that for an hour. I couldn't let her go, she would just assume it was some nefarious reason to hang up on her. I had to let her get this out. I had to wonder, though. She definitely was getting worse as she got older. Was this my fate too?

I do get depressed at times.

Day 7, Tuesday Sept 21ˢᵗ

I was sitting at my desk going through some of my other cases in a vain attempt to catch up. My squad phone rang. "Derik, it's your turn."

"What? Like fuck it is, I got the last one," he laughed.

"No, I just made a call, so it's your turn."

"Making a call doesn't count as taking a call."

"Just answer the fucking phone." I was trying to read some documents.

As he took the call, he threw a paper clip at me to get my attention holding up one figure. "Ok, great thanks, man, we'll get back to you." He hung up with a big smile. "Easton's car's been found. It was torched on a side road near Houston."

"Texas?" Maybe it was a car jacking after all. No, that made no sense. They take cars like his to the Middle East, not burn them.

"Yep, that was Houston police. The remains were impounded a few days ago..."

"Remains? They found a body in the car?" I said surprised.

Derik laughed. "No, the car, Marg. It was a burned out shell. It took them this long to get the VIN off the engine block. This means Easton's out of state. So, this is an FBI issue now."

"Swell! Fuck the FBI. Last time they took one of my cases I never got any credit. Not until we confirm he is out of state do we even think about calling the FBI. For all we know someone stole it for a joy ride."

"OK. But what do we do with the car? Send it up here?"

"No. Call them back and see if the GPS is in tact, and ask if they can sit on it until we're done here. Tell them we think it was stolen."

Derik did call back, but the car was nothing but a melted shell. Thus the GPS was also destroyed. That's why we didn't find it.

"So," Derik continued. "He must have someone with him. There's no way he'd walk the hundred miles to Houston. Someone drove with him there and drove him back."

"You're assuming he drove the car there. If he did, he would have used his cell phone to communicate with that other person, right?"

"Makes sense."

"But you still have nothing on his phone, right?"

"Dick all. He could have used a disposable."

Didn't make sense. Now, assuming he was out there, what was Easton doing in Houston? Who was he with? I don't like more questions than answers, because it means you're going backwards, not forward in your investigation.

I asked Derik to call Insur-Data to get a list of all events Easton had attended in the last year.

Later that day we got Easton's personal financials. He had an American Express credit card. Lots of use was on it prior to his disappearance. But there it was. Two, and only two, records since he disappeared. One on the fourteenth, for a flight from Tampa to Grand Cayman Islands. Then another on the fifteenth from Grand Cayman to Rio de Janeiro in Brazil. Then nothing.

"Derik, look at this," I pointed out the two entries.

"Looks like that's where he is," Derik said. "Guess I was right about the car after all."

Smart ass.

"Brazil? But why? How? There's no other cards listed with any use after the fifteenth. And only two on this card," I pondered.

"So," Derik shrugged.

"Soooo, why just two? If he has other cards we don't know about, why would he use this card for these two and give us a trail? It's been days. No credit card use for food, gas or motels. Nothing, except these two. Why?"

"Cash? He didn't want to leave a trail. If he used his card we would know his route and where he might be going. We could intercept him if he left a trail. He's used cash."

If that was true, he was deliberately trying to get out of the country without being traced.

"And airlines generally don't take cash for tickets," I realized.

"So he had no choice there. By the time we got that transaction he was gone."

"Looks to me like he's taken off," Derik said. "Maybe these two credit card records are his way of saying 'fuck you' to us and his family."

"Swell," I said shaking my head. "This makes no sense. He ditches and burns his car in Houston, then flies to Brazil going to the Grand Caymans first. How did he get from Houston to Florida? Why did he go to the island first?"

"He rented a car?"

"He went to Grand Caymans for a car?" I said looking at Derik sideways.

"No, he rented a car to get to Florida from Houston."

"Hmm, we'd see that on his card. There's nothing. They won't take cash as they need the ability to charge a card if there's an issue with the rental."

"Either he has a card we don't know about, or someone else paid for it. Again, this seems to confirm my original suspicion. He had an accomplice who drove him from his burned car."

"Maybe. Maybe. But I still don't understand the stop over in the Caymans."

"He went to get something?" Derik said.

"Yeah. To get something. But what?"

"Money? Maybe he had an off shore stash of money?"

Bloody hell. That had to be it. "I want you to call and fax photos of Easton to the airline in Florida. Let's get a positive ID."

"Soon as we get that, and we confirm it's Easton on the manifest, we'll have to call the FBI," Derik said.

"Yeah, fuck, yeah. Swell! For now, we keep this to ourselves, got it!"

Now why was he in Brazil? Where was he getting his money from?

"Derik, you pulled the company financials?"

"Not all of it, we got the bank statements and the income tax forms, but not the company investment holdings. Easton's father is still refusing access to those records. We'll have to get a warrant for them. Soon as we get all that I'll send it off to the forensic accounting guys up stairs."

"You find me one penny missing. He's gotta get his money from somewhere. Are there any large withdrawals from his personal accounts?"

"Let's see." Derik looked through the folder. "He has three personal accounts, just the normal monthly payments for the usual. The wife has one of those accounts. The last time a big withdrawal was a month ago, a debit payment for a ring. Five grand."

"Get what you can, I'm going call to Insur-Data and talk to Easton's father about this."

The company was still in disarray, but coping. It took pressure, and had to wait an hour, before I got a call back by Easton senior. I told him what we'd discovered.

"I don't believe it," he said forcefully. "My son would never steal from us. He would never burn his car. He loved that car. It was his symbol of his success. Something bad has happened."

"We have no evidence of foul play. We have evidence, sir, that your son went to Brazil with a stop over in the Grand Cayman Islands. Any reason why he'd do that? Did he have some event with someone?"

"Brazil? How do you know he flew to Brazil?"

"We have two credit card records for two flights. Nick's credit card was used for the airfare."

"It must be a stolen card. He wouldn't go anywhere like that without telling us. Have you located his cell phone yet? All I get is his answering service."

"Nothing on that yet. He had no business to be at in either place?"

"No, if he did he would use the company credit card for expenses. I've seen no transactions by Nick since he disappeared. Something's happened to him. Have you even investigated that possibility yet?"

Of course we hadn't yet. There was no reason for us to suspect this without any evidence.

"You did mention you had threats. You still think it was a former employee?"

"I don't know. Isn't that your job to find out? Maybe it was, maybe it wasn't. But you know how bad the city is for crime."

"If your son was subjected to crime in the city, his car wouldn't have ended up in Texas."

"Look, detective…" that wasn't a compliment tone, "…you need to do your job and find my son! He's not taken off with any company money, and I find it insulting you'd even assume that."

"We want to check your books," I said firmly. "You still refuse to give us access to your investments. I have to say, Mr. Easton, that doesn't look good. Looks like your hiding something."

He was silent.

"Do I have to get a warrant, sir, or will you freely show us your son didn't steal from the company?"

He was silent again. I was put on hold. He came back a few minutes later. He made a call to his accountant, and told them to make our books available to us. "There, detective, we have nothing to hide. Find my son. I'm convinced someone has done him harm."

Day 8, Wednesday Sept 22nd

Derik came in behind me, and dropped a folder on my desk.

"You should look at this I found in the financials. Whitman sued Insur-Data for wrongful dismissal and won. I went and got the court transcript. He's the only one of the people fired who sued."

Oh, that was interesting. How come Easton's father didn't tell me about that? I opened the folder and looked through the papers. "How much did Whitman win?"

"Judge awarded a fair sum, two year's pay. No where near the two mill he was asking for."

"Two mill, that must have puckered Easton's asshole."

I went through the court transcript and evidence. The company claimed Whitman screwed up a critical account. Regardless,

Whitman nailed it pretty quick in one day and the judge made his decision. The nail in the coffin was Easton lied to the court about promising Whitman would have a job for life. Easton denied he promised anything, not even full time employment, and claimed Whitman pestered him for full time work.

In the documents was a letter from Easton to the Federal Government admitting the life time promise of work so Whitman could get a tax refund for moving expenses to get closer to Insur-Data while still working for the State. He moved a year before retiring from his State job as an IT manager and programmer.

The judge didn't have kind words for Easton. "So, either you are lying to me or you lied to the Federal Government. Which is it?" the judge asked Easton. According to the transcript Easton said nothing. The judge accused Easton of using people and throwing them away.

This was not the picture I was getting of Easton from his family and coworkers. Maybe that event changed him. But old habits die hard.

More than ever I needed to talk to Whitman. I called again. No answer.

I had just got off the phone when our division commander came into the squad room with an announcement.

"Listen up everyone. Get into your gear. Pick up an M4 from the armoury. Met me at the front door."

"What's going on, sir," someone said.

"A riot's broken out with striking garbage men. Get moving everyone!"

Oh, shit. I'd never done this before. Must be something nasty.

I got my vest, helmet and headed to the armoury.

M4's are the common rifle for the Chicago Police. I'd fired it once, when I was a cadet. Now they want me to brandish this thing as if I knew what I'm doing? I didn't even remember how to load a magazine!

We were likely just sabre rattling. A show of intimidation.

It was no small riot. The entire width of North LaSalle Street in front of the Mayor's office was packed with humans, from West Madison Street to West Lake Street, three full blocks. Other unions were present in solidarity with the garbage men.

Our job was to set up a perimeter around the Mayor's office.

A convoy of a dozen school busses took us through a mass of angry mobs as they pounded on the windows. We disembarked at the back of the building, then made our way as a formation through to the front doors.

We formed a human barrier as we spread into LaSalle Street parting the way. The Mayor was right behind us, like some Moses parting the Red Sea. He was definitely the sort who thought he was the god of our city. Glad I didn't vote for him.

All night our show of force had a firm grip of the situation. By midnight, only the die-hard protesters remained, keeping warm with fires in forty-five gallon drums.

I was allowed to go home around 1am. Finally. I was scared shitless. I ended up right on the front line. Only a shield and facemask between me and screaming angry protesters. They spat at me. They threw food at me. They swore at me.

I found it very paradoxical. I was paid by the city. They were also employees of the city. The city was at civil war.

When I got back to the precinct to unload my gear, I heard a number of regular beat cops complaining about the whole event. One guy said his brother-in-law was in the crowd.

This could come down to our guys refusing to be part of quelling a riot. I wondered when that tipping point would be reached. I hoped I wasn't around when that happened.

Day 9, Thursday Sept 23rd

Between Derik and I, we contacted the rest of the living who were fired, except the one who appeared to have left the country. Those who we talked to told the same story. Easton was a user of people. Promised the world to lure them from other occupations, then dropped them when he had no use for them. Many were bitter, but had moved on.

We queried each as to if they threatened the company or Easton personally. Each denied of course. Easton senior admitted he didn't have any hard evidence. No emails, no letters of intent to harm. Just phone calls from a few frustrated at losing their jobs.

I talked to the wife of the man who committed suicide. She lived in Albany and had remarried. She told me over the phone that her husband was totally devastated by being fired after being promised a good job at Insur-Data. He left a good job, with benefits and a retirement fund to work for Easton. He couldn't find work in his field, not even out of state. He was too old. They lost their house, which was the last straw. Her husband walked in front of a train.

I was beginning to wonder, had someone killed Easton in revenge after all? It would be a powerful motive, especially in this economy where unemployment was the highest since the Dirty Thirties. If I found this was the case, I'd have to tell Chief David and he would reassign the case to homicide.

However, the tickets to Brazil showed otherwise. If that was Easton, then he was alive and well. But for some reason was not contacting his family. If that were true, I'd have to contact the FBI.

No way. I wanted to see this through. I had to sort this evidence out.

Whitman was the last person alive I hadn't contacted. Whitman either didn't answer his phone, or he'd been away. I had to drive up and check. One more phone call before I trekked all the way up to Earlville.

I was just about to hang up on the fourth ring when, "Hello."

"Mister Whitman?" I asked.

"Yes".

"This is detective Marg Cunningham of the Chicago Police Department."

"Ok. And you are calling me for what?"

Weird question. Guess I needed to talk to you, moron.

"You were fired from Insur-Data in two thousand and one, correct?"

"Shit, I hadn't thought about that in years, and now you bring it up. Thanks for spoiling my lunch," he said angrily.

Hmm, that reminded me, I hadn't had anything yet either. Busy life, poor eating habits.

"I need to ask you some questions," I said.

"About what? What can I possibly tell you about that slimeball?"

Slimeball? Guess he didn't like Easton much even after ten years.

"Sir, your name came up in our investigation. So, either I come and pay you a visit, or I will make sure you come down here and visit us in our interrogation room. Take your pick," I said. There was a pause.

"When? I was just about to sit down for lunch." The voice sounded reluctant.

"Today, I can drive up now."

"Hmmm. What's this actually about?" he asked.

I wasn't going to tell him about Easton over the phone. I needed to see people's body language when I questioned them. Body language says more than what people are saying.

"We don't discuss cases over the phone," I said.

"Well, I'm not going to agree to a blind date unless I know something as to why I should agree. I haven't had any dealings with that shitbag in ten years. I have nothing to share."

Yep, he still holds a grudge. A ten yearlong grudge. Sounds permanent.

"I need to be thorough," I said.

"It'll be a short visit. Four hours of driving you know."

"On the city's dime, not mine," I said.

"I guess I have no choice do I?"

Fuck no he didn't. If he didn't agree I'll come up anyway.

"Nope," I said.

"Fine."

"I'm on my way." And I hung up.

Derik showed up just I had gathered my things to leave. "I

contacted Whitman, heading up there now. Take any calls for me. Oh, and anything on the company books yet?"

"We need a warrant for the investments. The investment company won't let the portfolio out without one. Easton's father is adamant."

"Well, fucking get one, shit man."

That's not like Derik, he's usually on the ball. But then again, why would a company agree to see their books, no warrant, but not investments? You know they have something to hide. What morons. It really pisses me off when companies have money to hide from me, don't want me to see their books, demand a warrant, which they are then forced to show me the books. And then I get to nail their asses. I'll bet Easton has fucked off with some of the company's investments.

"For a missing persons? I have to go in front of a judge and get a warrant for company financials because of a missing person? Right," Derik said.

Walking out the door I yelled back at Derik. "Pick the right judge. Get Zimmerman when he rotates through, he never turns down one of my requests. I'll expect that warrant in the morning. I'll be gone the rest of the day."

Nice town Earlville. I'd never been there before, but then again, I don't get out of Chicago much. Just to see my Mom now.

Whitman was just out of town, along a river. It was a very small house but on a nice sized lot though. The house was a 1950's ranch style with yellow brick siding. He was home. There was a small compact car, an old model, in the drive.

He answered the door before I could knock. I was greeted by an elderly man, early sixties maybe. He looked the typical short stature computer geek type. His hair was full, mostly grey, not long, but not recently cut. He also hadn't shaved in days. He was wearing a t-shirt with a big parrot on the front, and old worn blue jeans. He looked like he'd been worn out. Life was heavy on him. He looked in good shape, however. Like he at least worked out to some extent.

The small bungalow was a mess. Though it looked like he tried to clean up a bit. Dirty dishes filled the kitchen, even on the floor. A large tan dog, and I mean LARGE dog, filled the sofa. It didn't even get up to greet me, just lifted his head, and a laboured quick flap of his tail. That was one huge head! Bigger than mine. He had wonderful drooping eyes on a black face, with long floppy ears. His paws were huge, hanging off the sofa. The dog's name was Rug. Seemed fitting.

There was also a large white bird on the back of the same sofa, eating some bread. Crumbs were falling onto Rug's back, but he took no notice. A huge cage was in front of the living room window. The main door to the cage was open. Inside was a large grey parrot. Of course I didn't know what these birds were until Whitman introduced me to them all. Animals aren't my thing. Dad's fish were Dad's fish, that's why I took them. I like animals, just never had a pet even as a kid. Too dirty my mother told me. As if fish weren't dirty. But that was Mom.

When I asked about the cage door being open he said, "I don't cage my friends." Would he cage his enemies I wondered.

On the wall over the couch was an M1 Garand rifle, which had been deactivated, or so Whitman said. It was his father's in WWII. Under the rifle hung medals and a photo of a US Army Staff Sergeant. Whitman's father he said. His father won the Distinguished Service Medal, the Silver Star, and three Purple Hearts. According to Whitman his father was involved in rescuing Patton's son from a prison camp. I knew who General Patton was, but didn't know his son was in a German POW camp.

Over the shrine of military paraphernalia was an American Flag. Whitman said it was the flag his father erected in a German town when they occupied it. I could see tears in Whitman's eyes after explaining his father's heroism. Indeed, it was a powerful story, but I had a job to do.

On the dining room table at the back end of the living room were all kinds of computers and equipment scattered around. A bookcase against the wall was loaded with technical computer and science books. Not just simple science books, these were in depth science texts: geology, physics, cosmology, evolution. He had the whole gambit. This guy was well read.

The house needed touching up, it definitely showed its age.

Some places the walls where re-plastered but not sanded or painted. Other places needed plastering. Even the floors needed refinishing. Whitman said the house was his father's and paid for.

We sat at the kitchen table, at least that was clean. The sink was full of pots, something was on the stove, which hadn't been cleaned in a while. Some plates were clean in a rack beside the sink. The backs of the wooden chairs had been chewed, I suspected from his birds.

Whitman poured me a glass of ice-cold water from a jug that was in the fridge. I was relieved it was a clean glass from the cupboard. I could see inside the fridge. For a double door fridge it looked pretty empty.

Time to get down to business. Whitman sat opposite me, arms on the table, hands clasped together.

"Where were you on September the tenth?"

"Wait. I don't understand. Why are you asking me about a specific date? What's shithead got to do about that date?"

"Mr. Whitman, I ask the questions," I retorted. "So, where were you on September the tenth?"

"I was in the mountains around Kamloops," he said with out making a move.

"In Canada?"

"There's no other Kamloops."

Smart ass.

"How long were you there?"

"Two weeks, I came home yesterday."

"You have proof?"

"I flew American Airlines from O'Hare to Vancouver. I didn't stay at any hotels, I camped in the Mountains."

Camped in September? Don't people normally camp in the summer? "You went camping in September?"

"Best time, few people. I prefer fewer people."

He's a loner.

"When did you leave?" I asked.

"The eighth, no the seventh."

Thus, he was gone two weeks. Then it dawned on me. "What did you do with your animals?"

He looked at me sideways, as if my question was out of line. Then he answered.

"Obviously, I sent them away for the two weeks. My wife took Rug, and I belong to a parrot group, and we look after each other's birds when we have to leave."

So, he wasn't around when Easton disappeared. Great, another dead end. Ok, let's get his story.

"You started with Easton when he started his company?"

"Yes, I was working in the IT department for the State at the time. On weekends I worked writing software for a bit of extra money. We had a mutual friend who I did a program for. I was asked to a meeting with Fucknuts…"

Fucknuts, oh yeah, this guy is bitter.

"…to lay out how to model his business so he could get it started. I did it over a weekend, and he hired me on the following Monday to build his system. He even paid me in advance, a month's pay up front."

"That was generous," I said. This guy must be good at what he does, or did.

"At the time I thought so, yes. After that he kept pestering me to work for him full time. I told him I'd get too much of a hit on my pension.

"After three years, the State was in financial crisis and willing to let people go early if they wanted. I did the math. His pay plus my pension, guaranteed job with Insur-Data for at least twenty years, I was set from what I could see. Boy was I naive."

"I don't understand, you said three years, yet you only worked for him for two years before you retired."

"No, I worked for his company for three years before I retired. We did contract work for insurance companies. He got enough business to start the company," he said.

Ok, that didn't make sense; I had him with the two jobs for two years, not three. "I have your tax records that you worked for both for two years not three."

"It was three years, give or take a month, spanning over two calendar years, hence two years of tax records."

"No, three years should be three tax years. I don't understand."

"Ok, I'll be honest, it was a long time ago. In the first year, well not a whole year, about nine months, he paid me under the table, cash. He was strapped for money, and we agreed to a lower rate of pay if I didn't declare it on my taxes."

"That's illegal."

"Then call the IRS and have me arrested."

I made sure I got that in my notes. "No, I won't call the IRS."

Still, Whitman made no move, same pose at the table.

But then something happened to cause Whitman to be fired.

"Yes," he said. "And I sued his ass. Didn't get what I wanted, but the judge did give me a good settlement. Drove Fuckhead up the wall. He stormed out of the courtroom." Whitman showed a smile that time.

"You sued Easton for wrongful dismissal," I said.

"No, breach of contract. But the only way he could fire me was to frame me for a mistake I didn't do."

"Their records said you screwed up a client's project. Something about misinformation in the data and wrong analysis."

Whitman shook his head, "Liars. It was a set up."

"You know that for a fact?" I asked.

"Yes. I knew the data. I knew how it was set up, how much data that was entered, and how it was analysed. I had completely automated the analysis process. My coding would fire the Stored Procedures, dump the recordsets into Excel, and then add the appropriate type of equations depending upon the data type."

I watched Whitman's body language, no move in posture, but his face was a person very angry. I was writing this all down.

"So I knew nothing new had been added in weeks," he continued. "Then out of the blue Shithead asked for a rerun. That made no sense; we were done with the project the previous week. The report had been sent to the client. But he claimed they wanted a rerun. So I did. Which was nothing more than selecting the client on the screen from a list, and pressing the 'Run Analysis' button. I sit back and watch the Excel spreadsheet, graphs and all, get generated by my code. It was a beautiful work of art. What would take me an hour or more by hand, took less than a minute. Shithead encouraged this. He always said work smart not hard.

"I didn't bother to look at the results, how could it have changed? So I emailed the spreadsheet." He paused as if getting what's next out was painful.

"Next day he storms into my office and tells me to clear my desk and leave."

He paused again. I could see he was keeping his emotions back. This was clearly disturbing for him.

"We had quite the argument, you can well imagine. He claimed the analysis was wrong and the client was furious. His second in command was with him. They escorted me off the premises.

"So I sued. He did promise me employment for life. Did his father tell you that?"

Why did he bring his father up? What did he know of my interview with him, how could be possibly know about that? "His father? What does his father have to do with anything?"

"Any investigator worth their value would have already interviewed people at the company before now. I assume you talked with his father about me. And what is it exactly you are investigating? Did Shithead finally get caught doing something illegal?" he said.

Smart guy. But I didn't want to tip my hand about Easton just yet.

"No, he never said anything about you. But I did see that in the court transcript. You made the case and won. You clearly retired early from the State to work for them."

"I had evidence I presented. It won the case."

"Saw that. Pretty clear to me. So, you were angry?"

"Fucking right I was."

Now he finally moved. He sat back in the chair and folded his arms.

Time I took him off topic a bit and get some background on him. "You married Mr. Whitman?"

"I am, but separated." He showed me the ring still on his figure.

"When did you get separated?"

"Two years after Fucknuts fired me. I couldn't get another job, and the house was too expensive on my small pension and my wife's income. We were forced to sell the house. The lawsuit took two years, and that was rough on both of us. So she moved on. She blamed me for getting fired. I moved in with my aging father. He needed someone here anyway."

OK, I had one person fired who committed suicide, another who had a nervous breakdown and hospitalized, and this guy who lost his home and family. Easton left a trail of destruction. The next question had to be asked.

"You threaten Mr. Easton?"

"Yes, with the lawsuit."

"No, I mean verbally threaten him."

"Not my style. I wouldn't tip my hand like that. I'm sure his asshole puckered when he got served with a two million dollar lawsuit. That I would love to have seen."

Next obvious question. "You wanted to kill him?"

He leaned forward and looked me straight in the eye. "Damn straight I did. I wasn't the only one. So he's missing, that's what your investigating isn't it."

"I never said he was missing."

"Why else would you ask if I wanted to kill him? Have you found his body?"

I wasn't going to answer that. Of course admitting you wanted to kill someone, and actually doing it were two different things. "No crime wanting to kill someone," I said.

He was silent.

"Yes, I noticed he had a long list of people he let go. Big turnover. So, you wouldn't be unhappy if he disappeared."

He leaned back in the chair and crossed his arms again. "What do you mean by disappeared? You didn't answer my question, so I suspect you haven't found his body. Maybe he's run off with company money."

"What makes you think he's done something illegal?"

"From you. If he's not dead, but missing, then why else would you be investigating Shithead?"

"I never said anything as to why I was investigating. He could be dead for all I know."

I wanted to see any reaction to that. He just looked a bit confused.

"I'm confused then. Why would he be dead?" he said. "Did someone finally put him out of our misery? Wouldn't surprise me. Do you want to know the real reason why he fired me?"

"Something not in the court transcript?"

"Oh, yeah, because I had no evidence. Just a huge hunch."

"Share it."

Whitman moved forward again with his arms back on the table clasping his hands.

"He's a womanizer. Loves to have just women working for him. Just before my incident with him, which caused my firing, he had a woman come and evaluate the efficiency of his employees. She spent several weeks interviewing people, and going over projects. How long they took, etcetera. She interviewed me, and I showed her how all the software worked, how the data was stored in the database. She seemed quite impressed.

"I didn't put it together at the time, I was so mad. But when I was escorted out of the building I noticed she was in Easton's office. Thinking afterwards, she was done weeks ago, so why was she suddenly there? Why at that very time?

"I noticed when I was demonstrating my software that she understood it. She even made comments about ability before I demonstrated it. So she was clearly some kind of IT person, maybe even a programmer herself.

"I suspect Easton replaced me with her and set me up so she could get my job."

"Why would he do that if you did nothing wrong?" I asked. "Why would he set you up for a firing? That's the part I don't understand. Seems to me you were an important asset."

That would be illegal if he could have proven that, Whitman would have gotten much more in his suit.

"I havn't been there in ten years, but knowing Easton I suspect he's not changed. What's the ratio of female employees to male employees?"

I had to think about that. Then it dawned on me. "He has only one male employee, the rest are women."

"Of course. Did you notice one thing all those women have in common?"

"Other than being female, they're competent? Maybe, just maybe, he happens to have competent women employees."

"If only that were true. The one thing they all have in common is they all have big tits. Easton is a tit man."

Oh, give me a break. A tit man, who the fuck does he think he's fooling here. He was just being bitter, that's all. But I let him continue.

"He loves to surround himself with large breasted women. Every male person he had working for him, within a year, he replaced them with a woman with big tits. I think he took his inspiration from Charlie Wilson."

Who was Charlie Wilson? An employee we missed? We didn't miss anyone. Must be a friend of Easton's. I wrote the name down.

"I hadn't noticed." Now I'm going to have to go back to Insur-Data to see if those women there do all have big breasts. "Who interviewed you?"

"I don't remember her name. But I do remember she was tall and liked to show her well formed cleavage."

I think this guy had the fetish, not Easton. Glad I was properly covered. Though, I never saw his eyes go down to my chest, he was looking at me directly, or off to the side on occasion. But I do recall that their IT person was wearing a rather revealing top when I was there. That must be her. "She still works there, she's their IT manager, your job."

"I fucking knew it!" He leaned back against the chair throwing his hands up. That was the only time his body showed any emotion. He sat there shaking his head looking down.

"I'm going to have to be frank with you, Mr. Whitman. You sound rather sexist to me. How do you know he's a breast man?"

He leaned back forward and folded his hands again, as if the pose was his information pose.

"About a year before I was fired, I was going from my office into the lunch room. To get there I had to go through the conference room. Easton had six of his production managers on the floor. All six were women he had recently hired for new projects. He had moved the tables and chairs out of the way, and had them on the floor so he could look down their tops."

Now that was strange. I wrote this down.

"It didn't click at the time, I just thought it weird he would have them on the floor for a meeting and not at the table. But later I realized what he was doing. With their heads up and their breasts hanging down, you could see right through."

"That does sound strange."

"I also found pornography on his computer."

Well, that's not uncommon. Lots of men have porn on their machines, hell I caught a priest with it when I arrested him in my vice days. So what's new? He continued.

"Part of my job was to make sure files were backed up, and there were no viruses on machines. So I had to physically check them out. I usually did that either after hours or on a weekend, when they were not in use. That's when I stumbled on his folder full of nude videos of women. All with huge breasts. Many of the videos where people screwing."

This is a new side of Easton I hadn't heard about.

"But there's more," he said.

More, how much more could there be?

"He had affairs with several of the woman on staff. He also had affairs with women when he went on trips to various events around the country."

Holly fuck, now we *are* getting something new. "You know this for a fact?"

"Yes. I almost caught him and his personal secretary coming out of the woman's washroom. He forgot to zip his fly."

"Who was that?" I was ready to write a name. His dog came into the kitchen and flopped himself onto the floor beside me. I couldn't help but rub behind the ears. Rug really liked it.

"Sorry, I'm real bad with names. Just check who it was with his records when I was there. She came on board about two years before I was fired."

He waited for me to finish writing, then continued.

"I went on one trip with him. The one and only time. He used me as a showcase. When I explained how our methodology worked, it would woo the client. I went to many meetings in Chicago, but only one outside the city. That was Washington DC. It was a convention of small insurance companies and we were meeting with half a dozen potential clients.

"After the second meeting, I could see he was eyeing one of the women there from one of the companies. Big tits of course, with lots of cleavage showing. They were clearly making eye contact. That night he was not in his room. I found him the next morning for breakfast in the lounge. He said he was up early for a run. That was a lie. He never got to his room because around eleven I called his room about something.

"So, if I were you, I'd look at who he'd been with lately. He's likely taken off with someone. His wife is a real bitch, you know. She used to hound him all the time about not making enough money. I figured he'd leave her one day. You're looking for him, that's what this is about isn't it."

He's implying that Easton has taken off with someone. That may explain Brazil. It was possible, I guess. It would also explain how the car got burned, and how he got to Florida. Derik was right, again.

However, I didn't know he was screwing around. "I'll take that under advisement," I said back. I had to ask, "Did Easton know anyone from Brazil?"

Whitman paused, his expression was one of surprise that I would ask.

"So, he *is* missing. Interesting." He leaned back in the chair, nodding. "Not that I know of, his business was only in the US. Though in my last year he was looking to get business in Europe and Mexico. So by now he could have expanded to Brazil, it is a fast growing economy down there. I'm sure he'd try to tap into that.

"However, there's more that could have impact on your investigation," he said, moving back again to the table, with the same pose.

"There's more?" I asked.

"Have you checked into the company's books?"

"None of your business." Of course we had, but I couldn't tell him. We hadn't found anything unusual. Though we were still waiting for the company's investment portfolio.

"Do you know he has, or had, a shadow company with a silent partner? He was using that shadow company to buy homes around the university and then renting them out to students."

What? Derik hadn't found anything about that. But still, even so. "That's not illegal," I said.

"No, but sending fake invoices to Insur-Data for services not rendered is."

I stopped writing and looked straight into Whitman's eyes. "You have proof of this?" Now I was intrigued.

"Absolutely I did. On one of those computer update days, when no one was there, a Saturday if I remember, I had to update a new version of Windows on his machine. I accidentally double clicked on the Excel icon on the desktop. It opened blank, but you know under files where the last spreadsheets are listed?"

Of course, I know what a spread sheet is, what does this guy think I am. Whitman was a snoop.

"One of them was this shadow company. I opened it."

"That was illegal," I said.

"Then arrest me. Do you want to know what I saw or not?"

I stopped writing, and just looked at my pad. "What the fuck, go ahead." I started to write this down.

"He had billed, on a regular monthly basis, his own company for a total of some one million."

I stopped writing looked up at Whitman and asked, "And tell me you kept a copy of that file."

"No, at the time it was none of my business," he said.

Damn, what a scoop that would be. So Easton was scamming his own company. I'd get Derik on this right away. I'd call Derik, but I didn't want to expose too much to Whitman. I'd wait until I got into my car.

"Do you have any more?" I asked.

"Not that I can think of off the top. It has been ten years, likely much has changed since I was forced out."

"OK, so I want to thank you for your time and information. It was most helpful after all wasn't it?"

"Well, good luck finding the prick. I hope he's done something really stupid and you lock his ass up for a long, long time.

"We'll find where he is."

"Not if he's in Brazil. I suspect, maybe I'm wrong, but I'd bet the US has no extradition treaty with Brazil. If he's gone there. That's why you asked about it."

True, but I wasn't going to acknowledge that. I finished the glass of water, stood up and said, "I'm going to take this back to the office and see what I can find out. Thank you for your time. Should you remember more me please call me." I passed him one of my cards. "Nice parrots by the way." I had to carefully step over Rug, as he didn't move at all for me to get by. He just snored and grunted.

"Definitely not a guard dog," I said.

"No, we don't need guard dogs here. We have no crime at all. No one locks their doors here. This is a really nice neighbourhood."

Better than my shithole apartment then. Too bad it's so far to Chicago.

When I left the house, I realized it was too damn late to go back to the office. I needed to get some sleep, and find out how Mom was doing.

I had to eat first. I had a throbbing headache, which happens when I don't eat. I wonder if I was getting diabetes. That's all I needed to complicate my life. I stopped in town at the Sunshine for dinner. Nice place, gave me time to make notes and have a good meal for a change.

I ordered their pork chops with mushrooms and onions special. It was the best I'd ever had. Hell, it was the best meal I'd had since I couldn't remember. Ironic, or maybe some kind of sign, the dinner's check came with a small Whitman's chocolate.

I got home late. There was a note taped to my door. It read: "No more room for garbage, take across road to basketball court."

I saw that as I came in. The court was full, some three feet high, of garbage bags. I could smell the stench as I drove by. And that was just the first week of the strike. Guaranteed the mayor was going to do something. This wasn't healthy.

Day 10, Friday Sept 24th

Arriving at my desk, Derik looked up and said, "How did the interview go with Whitman yesterday?"

"Good," I said. "He told me stuff the wife never told me about. Maybe she doesn't even know about."

I sat down and opened Outlook to see my email.

"So, you're going to keep me in the dark?" Derik said.

"What?" My focus was on my new mail.

"What did Whitman tell you?"

"Something puzzling. Do you know who Charlie Wilson is?"

"Why, is he an employee of Insure-Data?" Derik flipped through papers. "I don't see anyone of that name."

"Something Whitman said…"

"Do you mean Congressman Charlie Wilson?" came from behind

me. Arthur, two desks back, did the asking. Art was about to retire. Hell, he should have retired years ago. He reminded me of Fish on the old Barney Miller sitcom. That was my Dad's favourite cop show.

"I don't know. Why would Whitman make a comment about a Congressman?" I asked Art.

"Wilson isn't a sitting congressman, he was in Congress in the seventies and eighties."

"What the hell would a Congressman from decades ago have to do with this case?" I was really confused.

"How did he mention Wilson? What was the context?" Art asked.

"Something about Easton having big chested women working for him. Being inspired by Wilson."

"Ah, yep. Wiki Wilson, what you need should be there."

I did. Wow, looks like this Wilson character single-handedly defeated the Russians in Afghanistan. Oh, there it was:

Wilson was a self-proclaimed "ladies man" and the news media reported about his exotic bedroom complete with hot tub and handcuffs where he spent romantic affairs.

Yep, Wilson also had female only employees and escorts to important events. And I thought such had long disappeared. Ok, so Whitman was saying that Easton was a ladies man. I expected women wouldn't fall for that crap today. Guess a few still linger. But Whitman was there ten years ago, was Easton still a womanizer? Some habits are hard to change. If she knew, then his wife lied to me. There was no way she would not know about this.

I also almost forgot. "Derik, can you find out any other business or holdings of any other companies Easton was involved with?"

"I'll get right on it."

I missed a call on my cell. The nursing home called. I returned the call to horror. Mom was in a coma, she suffered another stroke. I did talk to Aunt May. I headed for the door.

"You leaving, Marg?"

"What?" I said in a daze.

"You going to the home?"

"Yeah, I can't concentrate on my cases right now."

"You have a meeting with the chief today," Derik said.

"Swell." I turned around and headed to David's office. I passed one of the other guys coming out as I slithered in.

"Marg," David said, "you're not scheduled until this afternoon."

"I need to go home. Mom's had another stroke."

"Oh, I'm real sorry. But you don't want to head out just yet, the traffic will be brutal. In the meantime, get me caught up on your cases."

I explained them all leaving Easton to last. David was intrigued.

"I've been getting calls all week from his wife."

I was surprised. "You didn't pass them on?"

"No, 'cause I know you hadn't gotten too far with your investigation. I told her he was still our top priority."

That was a lie, of course, we have to tell that to all our families who are in the queue.

"She got real nasty," David continued. "Real bitch. She swears someone killed him. You don't agree I gather."

"No, I have no evidence of that."

"Well, she won't stop calling. At some point you're going to have to talk to her."

"I will when I get more evidence."

"So you need some more time."

"Yes."

"Shit. In spite of my better judgment… OK, I'll give you another two weeks. But no more. Now go see you mom, my prayers are with you."

I gave a small smile, then left.

Day 11, Monday Sept 27th

Monday, another day I have to think about Mom.

I went on the weekend, stayed in a motel. Mom was transferred to the hospital. She didn't wake up at all. The doctor wasn't sure she ever would. The doctor said she would call me if anything changes and I should go home.

Consequently, I wasn't in a good mood when I showed up in the squad room.

Derik was just returning from the video room and met me in the hall.

"I watched the video," he said.

"The what? What video?"

"The ones from Easton's building."

"They had video cameras? That's great."

"Well, not really."

My heart sunk.

"Seems there was only two cameras, one on each corner, both of which faced the main parking lot. Easton always parked at the side of the building. All it shows is him, the last to leave, around 10:15pm."

"Nothing else?"

"Nope. Not even a shot of his car leaving, the far camera wasn't looking in the right direction."

A dead end.

Derik did have good news, however. He found Easton's silent partner: Roberto De Luca. He was a well-known real estate scammer with large holdings of homes and business malls. He'd been indicted a number of times for fraud, corruption, money laundering, to name a few, but nothing ever stuck. We call those people 'frequent flyers'.

What was Easton doing with this scum? I read the documents. Seems the two of them owned a company, Chicago Student Housing Corporation, where they were in possession of a dozen homes. They rented them out to university students. The company existed five years before Insur-Data. Whether Easton was involved then can't be verified. Formally, Chicago Student Housing Corp. was owned by a numbered company wholly owned by De Luca. But government documents showed Easton as the only other equal shareholder of CSHC.

Not only that, this numbered company invoiced Insur-data on a monthly basis. We had seen this when we went through the company's books, but thought nothing of it at the time. Records of CSHC also show some five million in dividends was paid to those two shareholders since Chicago Student Housing Corp started.

Whitman was right. Easton was skimming money from Insur-Data, likely to an offshore account, and using CSHC to do that. Hence, Easton's credit card being used for a flight from Florida to Grand Cayman. That's where he must have funnelled the money. He went there to get it, likely not alone, and then parked himself with whom ever in Brazil.

That was our new theory anyway. It just happened to fit the facts. Now, how to prove it. The problem was, if I did prove it, I'd have to give it to the FBI, which I wasn't looking forward to.

De Luca was easy enough to find. He had a website. And his mug, name and number was plastered on bus benches all over the city. We had to pay him a visit.

"There's more" Derik said. "The airport in Miami sent us the disk of people getting on the plane for Grand Cayman. They said they went through it. Easton got on the plane alone. However, the security photo is ambiguous. They can't positively identify Easton from the photo we sent. But they did confirm his passport."

"I'll take it to his wife. Maybe she'll…"

My Samsung made a little jingle. I opened it to see the email.

After a few minutes, Derik said, "Marg? Everything OK?"

I just shook my head. "Yeah, peachy." I put the phone away. "He may have disguised himself."

I wasn't concentrating.

"But use his credit card for us to see? Makes no sense."

"Anything's possible." I shrugged. "That's what we have to figure out."

"There's more."

"Go on, out with it, lad."

"Brazil won't send us any airport video. But they confirm Easton never got off the flight. No one by Easton's name came into the country. No one by Easton's name got on the plane in Cayman."

"Bastard assumed another name, using another passport."

"I don't get it," Derik said, shaking his head. "Why would he use his credit card but a different name for the flight? I don't get it."

Neither did I. Another dead end. Besides, even if that's where he went, we'd had no way of getting him back, let alone finding him. "Easton used his own credit card to buy the ticket. Can you get the name of the person on that ticket?"

"I was going to do that next."

"You do that, I have to head out." I left to walk down the street. I called who texted me, Pam.

"You texted me that Angel left you," I said.

I could hear her start to sob. "Yes. I found out he was with another woman. We had a big fight."

"Where are you now?"

"At a friend's. She said I can stay here if I need to."

"Are you going through with the pregnancy?"

"Of course, Mom."

"How are you going to raise a child on your own?"

"Well, I'm going to have to, aren't I? You won't want me to live with you."

"Besides the fact my place is a one bedroom apartment?"

"Fuck off, Mom, you know what I mean. I can't live with you."

The conversation didn't last long. Her mood deteriorated.

I went back to the precinct. We had to pay De Luca a visit.

When a cop interviews someone like De Luca one does not go alone. Not only did I take armed Derik along, I also put my sidearm on. Of course, we made sure our badges were hanging in plain view from our necks.

De Luca's office was right downtown Chicago on the twentieth floor. Cops also don't make an appointment to see De Luca, he would put any cop off for weeks if you let him. Hence, you just go there and barge in. I made sure he was in his office by having a black & white watch for to him enter the building.

We hardly acknowledged the secretary who was supposed to be the gatekeeper. We barged right into De Luca's office while he was on the phone.

"…ah, Gary, the fuzz just broke my door down. I'll have to call you back." He collapsed his cellphone. "Always a welcome to see Chicago's finest. How's old Dorski doing?"

That's his nickname for our Chief. David had tried a number of times to nail this guy to the wall, but he always managed to weasel his way out of anything we threw at him.

"Does he still sleep with that loaded 1911 under his pillow?"

De Luca was a heavy set, mid-fifties Italian looking man. To hide his balding he shaved his entire, ball-like, head into a high polish shine. His dark eyes, close together on either side of his beak, were very prominent on that shining globe. And he always had this Cheshire Cat grin on his face, the same grin on all his advertisement posters.

His office was, well, expensive. The walls were dark mahogany panels. The ceiling was done in cornices and medallions over the chandeliers. The floor was expensive Italian marble. Italian objects, small statues and paintings, adorned the atmosphere. Even a gold plated Beretta, behind glass, was hanging behind his desk.

On the right wall was a memento collection of 1930s Mob paraphernalia; photos of various prohibition era gangsters, newspaper clippings of convictions, etc. There was even a 1921 Thompson submachine gun hanging on the wall, with its drum magazine, that De Luca claimed belonged to Donnie Brasco, or John Dillinger depending on who he was trying to impress. A glass case was under all that, which contained a number of relics of the Prohibition era; bottles of booze, more guns, handcuffs, several ledgers, a baseball bat (which De Luca claimed was used by Capone, but it looked too new for that) and even Purvis and Ness photos with bullet holes in them.

The intricate oak desk, with his bulk behind, he claimed was from Capone's room at the Lexington Hotel.

Also behind his desk were various awards hanging on the wall. Amongst those were photos of him with politicians; the past four mayors we've had, the State Senator, and even the current State Governor. I wondered how much money De Luca gave to their campaigns.

No photos with the current mayor, however. That was interesting.

The full wall windows on the left had a wonderful view of the city with Lake Michigan behind it.

"Captain Doroszuk is doing just fine, thank you for asking. Better if we can nail your ass one day," Darik said.

"Ha ha, you guys keep tryin' don'cha." He laughed with his loud booming low voice, a voice any radio station would pay big bucks for.

"We're not here to arrest you Mr. De Luca," I said looking at Derik. I looked back at De Luca. "Do you know a Nick Easton?"

"Yeah, I know Nicky. What about him?"

"How long have you known Mr Easton?"

"Oh, I'd have to think about that. Maybe fifteen, sixteen years tops."

"What's your relationship with Mr Easton?"

"Why do you want to know this? What's Nicky got to do with me?" The grin transitioned into a stern look. He stood up and waddled his short chubby frame over to the bureau on the left wall under the window overlooking the city.

"We need to know your business…"

"You guys wanna drink?" he said cutting me off pouring himself a small glass of amber booze.

"No, you should know better than that. I want to know…"

"Nicky and I have a business arrangement, you know. That's all. Just some property we both own near the university. We rent it out to those poor students at very reasonable rates, you know."

"How generous of you," I said. He caught the sarcastic tone. He returned to his desk with the glass almost full. "When was the last time you spoke with Mr Easton?"

"Please, why don't you at least sit down. Take some load off your flat feet," he said with a laugh.

One could easily fall asleep in those chairs, quite irresistible. "Thank you. So when was…"

"Let's see…" he said cutting me off again, "I talk with Nicky about once a month. So it was some time late August, just to finalize some rent issues, understand?"

"Nothing since? No emails?"

"Nicky and I don't use email. Email today can be used as evidence, you know. Of course you do, that's how you tried to nail me the last time," he laughed. It's all a big game to him. "Therefore, I don't use email any more. And to answer your question, no. Not since then."

I'd love to ask him about the illegal billings of Insur-Data, but I needed to gather more evidence, since he would likely just deny anything about it. It just might be a way of finally nailing this guy's ass. But I'd have to wait. "Did you know Mr. Easton is missing?"

"Missing?" That perked him up big time, his smile evaporating into a grave expression. "Since when?"

"September eleventh."

"Nine-Eleven anniversary… You don't say." His pained expression grew.

"Do you know if he was seeing anyone?"

"What the fuck do you mean by that? He's devoted to his wife, you know."

Oh, I could see his lie a mile away on that. No Cheshire grin on his face.

"You don't think he's with someone else do ya? Nicky would never do that, oh no."

"Oh, come on Mr. De Luca, we know all about his extra-marital activities. Who was the last person you know Easton was seeing?"

He sat silent about that for a few seconds. He took a long drink from his glass, almost emptying it.

"Mr. De Luca, who…"

"He was seeing someone," he finally said in a low voice, and with a cat got caught look on his face. "Someone he met at a meeting we were at a couple months ago. I let the two of them use my penthouse for a night." He was playing with the glass on the desk, swishing the contents around.

"What was her name?"

"I can't recall," he said watching the waves of amber fluid. "I'm not big with women you know. Lucy something, Lucy, Lucy… Goddammit. Right on the tip of my tongue." He took another swig. "Something foreign. Mendez I think it was, or maybe Mendoza. I really can't recall. Very pretty woman. Nice pair of pillows she had. Some one paid a good price for those Danny DeVitos," he said laughing.

My stern stare at Derik stopped his chuckling. "Ok, Mr. De Luca, if you hear from Mr. Easton, please call me." I handed him my card as I got up to leave.

"Always willing to help Chicago's finest, detective…" he read the card, got up and walked in front of his desk, "…Cunningham. Cunningham. I thought I recognized you. You're Don Cunningham's daughter, aren't you?"

I turned towards him, "Yes."

"Wow, you know, your ol' man arrested me when I was seventeen. My first arrest. We struck a deal, though. I helped your ol' man with information, many times. I was sorry to hear he kicked the bucket." He turned to return to his seat, "Anyway, I sure hope you find Nicky alive."

Now why would he say that? I turned back, again. "Any reason why you think he's not alive? Do you have an insurance policy on him?"

That made him take a step back. He stopped and turned towards us before he could sit down. "Oh, no, please, whoa, don't get me wrong. Nicky and I have a perfectly good professional relationship. If he's left this earth anythin' he has with me goes to his wife, honest. I really do hope he's all right. But hey, this is a crazy world you know. No tellin' what can happen. As for insurance, not me, as I said. But his wife has a huge one on him. A couple mill he told me."

Derik wrote that down. "I'm on it," he said quietly to me.

"How much does Mr. Easton have in your partnership?"

That he didn't like. A dead serious look came over him. "Oh, that Marg, my dear, you'll have to get a warrant to find out." He lifted his last bit of booze in a toast.

"Good day Mr. De Luca," I said as we walked out the door.

"Why didn't you ask him about the shell company?" Derik asked.

"Not yet. I want you to find out all you can about that company first. Get a warrant for their books, if they have any. Let's get our ducks lined up first. Oh, and find this Lucy. I gotta get some coffee."

"I saw a Tim Horton's in the lobby."

"That Canadian crap? Awful. There's gotta be a Second Cup somewhere around here."

"But I like Timmy's. Besides, I've been buying you Timmy's for weeks, and you hadn't even noticed," he said. As the door to the elevator closed he chuckled, "Second Cup is Canadian too."

Later that day I had to go to court to hear a ruling on one of my cases. I was on cloud nine. They found the scum guilty of embezzlement and corruption and all because of my great work. He'd been missing for a month. He'd taken off to Canada, but I tracked him down in Calgary. He was a former city councilman, booted out last civic election. I took the rest of the day off to celebrate, alone. I even took in a movie, then continued my book to put me to sleep. It's times like that when one's spirits get up. I may even crack Eastman's case.

Day 12, Tuesday Sept 28ᵗʰ

Derik called me just as I was driving up to get my morning fix.

"Lucy Medina!" he said.

"What?"

"Her name, the woman that De Luca gave us, here name is Lucy Medina."

"How the fuck did you figure that out?"

"That will be a dollar sixty, please," the woman at the window said. But Derik said something at the same time I missed. "Just a second," I said to the woman, "Just a second Derik." I fumbled for change. "Here, thanks."

"There you go, have a nice day ma'am, and go get those scum!" she said.

Yeah, I go there every day and all the workers there knew me. "Sorry Derik, what did you say?"

"Her name is Lucy Medina…"

"I got that…"

"Yeah, I tried the other names, and no one fit. Then it dawned on me. She's likely a realtor. I was right."

"Wonderful, so you talked with her?"

"Yes, last night. She's married. She admits meeting Easton, but denies any involvement. She claims she knows nothing about him. I could hear children in the back ground, so likely not able to speak."

"Ok, good work, Derik, call her back and tell her to come to the precinct, no option. That'll intimidate her and give her some privacy."

"Will do."

Lucy was interrogated after her work. She broke down crying, shaking and trembling. It was all she could do to hold a glass of water. She admitted to the affair with Easton. She pleaded we didn't tell her husband. She gave us quite the itinerary on their meetings: days, places. Except none of that helped to find him. He was obviously not with her. The last time she saw him was the week before he disappeared. She was almost relieved he was missing. She said she couldn't break off the relationship; she just didn't have the heart to let Easton go. He made her feel so much more than her dull life gave her.

Swell, another dead end.

I got home very late to find Pam sitting in the hallway, with a suitcase.

"Hi, Mom," she said standing, almost in tears.

"It's 10:30, how long have you been waiting?"

"Don't know, couple hours I guess."

"What happened," I said unlocking the door.

We went to the kitchen, and poured us a pair of rum and cokes.

"Mom!"

"What?"

"I'm pregnant! Geeze!"

"Oh, right. Sorry. What do you want?"

"Milk will be just fine, thanks Mom."

"So, what's the story now?"

"I was thrown out of Kala's place."

"Why?"

"Her boyfriend wanted to move in. No room for me. I have nowhere to turn, Mom. I'll sleep on the coach until I can find a place of my own."

That was going to be awkward. I pressed the playback for the phone messages, force of habit.

"Miss Cunningham, this is Mini Rogers, Hank's wife, your realtor. I need to talk with you. There's no way we will sell your Mom's house at the asking price. Please call as soon as you can, thank you."

"Pam, go unload your things, give me a minute with this."

I dialled the number. The best that we got with offers was fifty thousand below asking. Some were as low as half the asking. Things in the market in Chicago had gotten that bad. I told her it was still early, and to keep it on the market. There was no rush to sell.

Actually, there was. My mother's savings might last her a couple months. Her survivor benefits didn't cover her at the home. Even though she was in the hospital, still in the coma, they were charging her for the empty room. It costs more than double to have her there than when she lived in her own house. Swell. Robbers.

Pam and I had a long conversation. It was completely civil. One would have thought we were best of friends. I wondered how long it would last. I wondered if this was because I was all she had left in the world.

Pam had to work early the next morning, and my next day was going to be full. We packed it in, in the same bed, for the night. Last time she did that was when she was ten.

She noticed the two books on the night table. "You're reading these?" She picked one up and read the back.

"Trying to, but don't seem to get the time."

"Look's interesting, when you're done I'd like to read them."

"At the rate I'm going that could be next year."

We chuckled.

I found my daughter again. It felt great.

We watched a bit of news. The mayor fired all the striking garbage men. He signed a contract with a private company to pick up all the garbage starting in the morning. He cited the increase in the rat population for the draconian action.

After that I watched something deeply disturbing. An economics professor was being interviewed about the severe rioting in several Middle East countries. He said that countries like Egypt, Syria, The Islamic State, and Yemen (I didn't even know where Yemen was) can't afford to pay for food imports. They imported more than 75% of their food requirements, he said. He said that should it get as bad as is possible, there could be a 95% cull in their populations over the next few years.

Dumbfounded, I stopped slurping on my rum and coke. I wondered if things were really starting to fall apart. And my daughter was pregnant; I could see in her eyes she was worried too. I clicked off the tube, enough of that.

Day 13, Wednesday Sept 29th

I dreaded making this call. I was going to have to confront Easton's wife about what we found out, and that he likely was having an affair. I've had to make such calls in the past. Reactions from wives ranged from uncontrollable sobbing, to, eventually, in the extreme, the wife murdering her husband, to a mild "who gives a shit".

I remember very well a case I will never forget. I was on the force only a few years, in blues. I got a call to go to a domestic dispute. The wife was told the day before that her husband was seeing hookers. According to the detective, she gave no reaction upon the news, almost as if she knew.

The next day she got her revenge. My partner and I were first on the scene. We came into the kitchen to find her at the table sipping on some tea. A large kitchen knife, dripping in blood, was on the table. She didn't even look at us when we came in the house. She just said, "that's the last time the prick will dip his stick in someone else."

I went in the bedroom. I was almost sick to my stomach. Her husband was all over the room, the walls, the ceiling, the floor. Most of his chopped up body was in the bed. His head was hanging, off the end of the bed, from a thread of spinal cord.

Later the detective told me she felt responsible. But had to inform the wife of her husband's infidelity. Now he was dead, and she was going to prison for the rest of her life. Well, maybe. Some, with good a lawyer, might get off. I handed this woman a card from a lawyer I new who could help her. She smiled at me when I handed it to her. Sometimes I have to decide which justice is better.

Derik had called Easton's insurance company about his life insurance policy. It was for death and disability. They were covered for life, several million. The insurance rep was clear, it didn't cover going missing, nor murder by the spouse.

He said, if Yvonne murdered her husband, they would investigate based on our outcome. That's pretty standard, especially today. The rep said they were getting many attempts to scam the system. The economics of the time, of course.

I got the courage and called Easton's wife. First, I told her we still had not found him.

"How can that be? It's been two weeks, does this mean he's dead?" she said. "Have you even found his car yet?"

"Yes, in Texas burned to a shell. No body inside."

"Texas, what was he doing in Texas?"

"We don't know for sure he was in Texas, but we do have two credit card records. One for an air flight to the Cayman Islands, and another from there to Brazil. Do you know why he would go there?"

"Cayman? We honeymooned in the Caymans."

"Did your husband have a bank account in the Caymans."

"No, not that I know of. We have a timeshare there, we spent a number of winters there."

"When was the last time?"

"Oh, I'd have to think about that. Maybe four years ago. Nick's been so busy lately we haven't gone on vacation together since then."

"Together?"

"Oh, I go on vacation by myself if he can't come."

"Where was your last vacation?"

"Hawaii."

"Does your husband do any business in Brazil?"

"Hmm, let's see. He went there about three years ago for a conference. He was hoping to get new business there. I don't think he got any business yet. Maybe that's where he is. He's gotten a new client, but hasn't been able to call me yet."

Two weeks on business and no calls? I don't think so. Next task, tell her about the women.

I explained, as we understood it, all the way up to Lucy. There was silence at the other end.

"Mrs. Easton, are you still there."

A low "yes" replied.

"We think your husband has left the country with another woman. Where you aware of his extra marital affairs."

The lie came back, "no." It was unconvincing.

In a monotone voice she said, "How do we prove he's gone to Brazil?"

"That's the tough part. If he's changed names it will be almost impossible."

"But he could be dead for all you know."

Worried about her insurance pay out? "We haven't ruled that out yet."

"How long until you can legally claim he's dead. I'll need his insurance. For the kids."

That last bit wasn't an afterthought. If he's disappeared with most of their assets, she is going to be in severe financial trouble. Likely lose the home. Definitely not get what she thinks she should get in this economy. Surely, she knows that.

"Mrs. Easton, if we believe he's left the country, we cannot make him legally dead."

"Do you're job and figure this out." She hung up.

Well, that was an interesting call. She didn't give a damn about Easton. All she cared about is to maintain her lifestyle. Going on expensive vacations alone, not even with her kids? Wow. Now I remember why I never bothered to get involved with someone. People are shits.

Then I wondered, was she having an affair on her vacations? Makes one wonder. Tit for tat. People are such hypocrites.

I was just about to call Whitman's wife when the Dragnet theme stopped me.

"Hello?"

"Ms. Cunningham, this is Doctor Rossiter. I have good news. Your mother has come out of the coma. She's awake and talking."

"Oh, thank you so much."

"She's been asking for you. Can you come up?"

"I can leave early. Thank you so much for this."

I called Whitman's wife first. What she told me was very disturbing. I was going to have to interview Whitman again. Maybe Easton wasn't in Brazil after all.

Day 15, Friday October 1st

Finally got some time today to get back at the Easton case. After interviewing Whitman's wife, I had to talk with him again.

I tried all morning to get him at home. It wasn't until after lunch he answered the phone.

I had planned to go back up to his place, but decided I'd call back and get him to come to our sweat room. Maybe I could shake him loose in there and get some emotion from him. He's gotta react to me knowing about his attempts, yes plural, to kill Easton.

Whitman showed up around three in the afternoon. I had Derik put him in an interrogation room. Of course, we leave them in there alone to sweat it out for a couple hours before going in.

Derik and I watched through the two-way mirror. Whitman looked around the room, spotted the camera, then looked into the mirror for a quick stare. He sat and folded his hands on the table.

"What's your game plan with him?" Derik asked. "Be his buddy, buddy?"

"Not sure yet. Not that. I'll just start off trying to get him to explain himself from what his wife told me."

"Hey, don't you have to meet with the Cap?" Derik said, looking at the clock on the wall.

"Damn it, your right."

While Whitman sweated it out, or so I thought, I had my regular Friday meet with Chief David. I brought him up to speed on Whitman. He was intrigued, but said I had only one week left to prove anything, and if it was murder after all, he'd have to send it up stairs. David stressed that, on the other hand, if Easton was in Brazil, it was to go to the FBI. He was inclined to do both. I had to plead just to get that week he originally promised.

Interrogation room chairs are deliberately uncomfortable. It increases the stress of the guilty, especially if they get thirsty or have to pee. Before I go in I look for these signs of stress: fidgeting, getting up and walking around. But not Whitman. He sat there, arms crossed, back against the chair with his eyes closed. Fucker was sleeping! We both waited long enough for him to move.

"What do you think?" I asked Derik.

"He's tired? Seems awfully calm to me."

"Too calm. I'll bet his wife told him. He's figuring out how to explain himself."

I came in, and sat across from him. He opened his eyes and moved towards the table folding his arms, just like he did at his place.

I placed a can of Coca-Cola in front of him. He shook his head. "No thanks. Trying to cut back."

"Your wife says you tried to kill Easton. Want to tell me about this?"

Ah! He looked stunned about that. I could see it in his eyes. He moved from his hands folded on the table, to lean against the back of the chair, crossing his arms over is chest. The defensive posture. He paused for a second.

"I was depressed," he finally said, eyes on the floor. "Big time. I couldn't find work. No one wanted to hire an over fifty, worn out, programmer when they could hire young people fresh with new skills. I'd have to go back to school and learn all the new stuff. Software changes are fucking faster than light, and ten years at Insur-Data got me out of sync with new stuff. I was too old to spend years learning all the Dot-Net syntax. So, I was out of work and I saw no future for myself." He looked back up and came forward again arms on the table.

"Easton was evil," he said with a stern look on his face, a face with anger in the back of it.

Past tense? "Was?" I asked.

"Was, is, what's the difference? He used people for his own pleasure and goals, which was to get rich at any cost to others. He was clearly of the school 'the end justifies the means'. So, I got it in my head to put a bullet in his brain."

He said he bought a handgun on the street, and waited in front of Easton's home one night. He wanted to gun Easton down in their front hall.

"But you didn't follow through. Why not?" I said, writing in my pad.

"Two reasons. I pride myself on not acting on emotion. Logic and reason rule. I've lived my life like that as long as I can remember. I plan everything I do. But at that time emotion had taken me over. Easton lives like that every day. He never uses logic or reason. He always acts based on emotion. Why else would you be a womanizer?"

Sure, not controlling one's sex drive is a problem for many people. It's why we have rape of small children. But, it's also about control in most cases. However, it seemed Easton didn't use his sexual influence to control these women. He was just horny.

"Sitting in the car, in the dark," Whitman continued, "with the pistol in my hand, I got an epiphany of logic. Yes, he would be dead. Yes, either I take my own life afterwards or go to prison for life, but who would ultimately suffer? My family. My daughter who would have to grow up without a father, who was a murderer. I respect my wife too much to have my face plastered on the eleven o'clock news."

Interesting, a potential murderer with a conscience.

"So, I went to the harbour, and threw the handgun into the lake. Then I went home."

"What if the maid had answered the door instead of Easton? How would that have gone down with you standing at the door with a gun?"

He sat there with a stunned look on his face. "Wow, you know, I never even considered that. Shit, that's likely what would have happened. I just assumed he would have answered the door. Not sure what I would have done in that case, I hadn't thought about that."

"And what about the kids in the house? He had two at that time."

"Yeah, I did think about that. He usually doesn't allow them to be upstairs unless it's for dinner. I guess you saw they have all their toys in the basement. But back then one would have been a newborn. You're right."

"Would you have killed the whole family?"

He went back into the chair quickly and put his hands up. "No, no. Absolutely not. No. It was him I wanted. His family wasn't to blame. If anything they were victims of him too. So, absolutely no. I would not have shot anyone but him. He was the only person on my mind."

"But they all would have been traumatized."

"Yes, just like Shithead traumatized the families of the people he fired. One guy killed himself, you know. Walked in front of a train. I liked him, he was a good hardworking guy. So sad for his family. But to Fucknuts, that was just collateral damage. He knew about it, too. That god damned cocksucker. They'd get over it, I heard him say. He said that about all those he fired."

"Would his family have gotten over you murdering their father?"

"I'm not sure the wife's grief would have lasted too long. Not once she got his life insurance and moved on."

Well, there's a contradiction. He just assumed the same thing about victims of violence as Easton. I looked up at him from my scribbling. "And that's when you got therapy?"

"Vicky told you about that too?"

"Yes, amongst other things."

"Like what?"

"I ask the questions here. How did the sessions go? Did they help your rage?"

"In a way, yes. The sessions themselves didn't. Psychiatry is hocus pocus nonsense. The guy was OK, nice enough young fellow. But after six sessions that were costing me a fortune, I figured out that he wasn't helping me at all. I had to help myself. I had to let the Shithead go."

Shrinks generally do well with weak-minded people. Whitman was definitely not weak minded. I could see a shrink wouldn't do much for him.

"So I did," he continued. "It took a long time, but eventually I got to the point where I would remember him once a month, not every day. Occasionally, a few things would remind me of those events. Mostly it had evaporated. Until you called. Now you've brought it all back up again. It's going to take me months to get over this, all over again. I thank you."

"Want to tell me about the radio controlled airplane?" I said, looking up from writing, waiting for an emotional response. He definitely was taken aback by that. But he shouldn't be surprised. He should know what I know if his wife talked to him about our conversation. I found it highly unlikely she wouldn't have called Whitman. I thought he would have been prepared for these questions.

Took a few seconds of repositioning his body for a reply.

"Yeah, another moment of lucid loss."

Another *moment*? Please. I had to confront that. "For a whole year? OK. So, tell me about it."

"Whatever my wife said, she always tells the truth."

"I need to hear it from you. All of it. Don't leave anything out."

He explained that he had spent a year at it. He made the barrel out of aluminium, because of the weight. He put a scope on the barrel, both of which pointed backwards, out the back of a four foot long radio controlled plane that he built for the task. That way the air friction was less. He explained in detail that the plan was to land the plane on the building across the road, line up the sights while Easton was on the phone, and take the shot. However, Whitman abandoned the attempt, finishing with "Besides, his artificial wife would get his insurance. You do know that's likely substantial."

He waited for me to respond to that. I didn't, just kept writing.

"I will need everything you have from that attempt, everything," I said.

"Can't, don't have any of it. I went out on the lake late one night and threw it over board, including the computer I wrote the software on, and all the tools to make the barrels and parts."

"Nothing's left then?" I asked looking up at him.

"I didn't want to leave any kind of trail back to me."

"Why would there be a trail? Were you planning some other retribution on Easton?"

"No," came a quick reply. "I just figured it would be safer all round to just dispose of all of it."

I finished writing this all down, "This was all before getting help, right?"

"Yes, my wife thought I was getting just a little obsessed. So she forced me to get help. You already know about that."

I paused for a few seconds before I changed tactic. I went on the offensive.

"I'm really pissed you missed these two key facts the first time we talked. You actively planned and experimented with killing Easton. You should have told me during our first interview. You do realize that even if you had nothing to do with his disappearance, this doesn't look good. You know that, right?"

"I have no obligation to incriminate myself or volunteer any information freely. Fifth Amendment and all that."

Unfortunately, he was right. He had no requirement to divulge anything. Not even answer to my direct questions. He could clam up, and walk out any time. Wouldn't look too good if he did. But it certainly did put another perspective on Easton's disappearance.

It was time to see if I could get a response. "Let me tell you what I think. I think you had something to do with Easton's disappearance. I think you murdered him. I think you disposed of his body." I pointed my index finger with every "I think". Without pausing I continued my blitz. "What have you done with Easton? Tell us where his body is. What else did you throw into the lake, Mr. Whitman?"

Whitman gave no response; he just looked at me sideways.

He sat there shaking his head and said, "So you're at a dead end. You can't figure out where he's gone, so you try to elicit a confession from me."

Well, that aggressive assault didn't work.

"Look, I understand you're stumped, and I do, no, I *did* look guilty. But I had finally put him behind me. Until, that is, you brought him back into my life. Which, I thank you so much for doing. It's going to take me years to get over him, again."

He moved forward, hands folder on the table, his eye's squinting.

"Let me explain something to you, so you understand the gravity of the damage he caused. My wife is my soul mate. We met at collage. Her and I were perfect together. I fully expected to grow old with my love. To spend at least fifty years together." His voice started to crack. "Because of my depression, she left me. That dream was extinguished because of that prick. That chasm in my life will never leave me."

Wow, an emotional outburst. Likely the most I'll get out of him. I hadn't realized how bad this was for Whitman. Tears were forming in his eyes.

His marriage was much like my parents. They deeply loved each other, and my father fully expected to live a long retirement with my mother. It never happened. I remember him crying about that on his deathbed. My mother was devastated losing her soul mate. I understood how this would be so depressing for Whitman. I actually started to feel sorry for him.

He changed tone interrupting my thought. His eyes pinned, and narrowed, his expression of anger clearly overflowed his posture.

"So, if you find that cock sucker dead somewhere." He paused a bit as a grin took over. "That would be nice. I wouldn't shed a tear over an evil person like him. Some people don't deserve to live, that is fact. I gave up trying to terminate him a long time ago. I figured something, or someone, would have had enough of him. That he would do something to someone else, and he would get his just deserts. 'Comeuppance' as the Brits would say. Maybe that's happened, or maybe he's taken off with someone else. That's *your* job to find out, not mine. I would really like to get on with what's left of my life."

Well, so much for that tactic. I had no evidence; no indication Whitman had anything to do with Easton. Back to square one.

"So, are you going to arrest me for attempted murder?" he finally said.

"No. You're free to leave," I said as I packed up my notebook. I stopped holding the door open and looked back at Whitman. "When you get home you will see that we have executed a search warrant. You'll find we've taken things." Then I left the room.

Derik was watching through the two-way window. "So, what do you think?" I asked him.

"If he's hiding something, then he's one helluva a cool cucumber. But I didn't see him gaze up to the left, not once. So, I think he's just a Spock and perfectly innocent."

"Bullshit. No way." I started to get frustrated. "No one is calm like that unless they're guilty. Look at him, Derik. He's almost completely detached. Too gawdamned composed. You know the psychology."

"I do, but I also know people are different. I had a case years ago, where this family had their car torched. It was sitting on the road, parked in front of their home over night. Well, we for sure thought the husband did it for the insurance. He was too cool under the light, just like that. Funny, he was a computer programmer too. But we couldn't break him. So we polygraphed him. Well, that needle was flying all over the sheet with every question, even one's we knew he was telling the truth. The man was cool and pokerfaced on the outside, but inside he was an emotional hurricane. Later we found out it was some kids in the area doing a number of vehicles. The point is, not all outwardly calm people are guilty. Maybe it's the breed. Something about those people make them good programmers? I don't know. But it doesn't mean Whitman's guilty."

"Swell," I said, disappointed.

"I guess one can sympathize with wanting to kill Easton, though," Derik said. "Losing someone like that is a powerful motive for murder. But with no evidence Easton hasn't done anything regarding his disappearance, what can we do?"

"You mean Whitman."

"Didn't I say that?"

"No you said, Easton didn't have anything to do with Easton's disappearance. You getting enough sleep there, Derik?"

"Shit, with all the load you've dumped on me, barely any sleep at all."

"Well, I'm going to dump more on you. Let's put a tail on him."

"For what?"

"I still think he's had something to do with Easton." Derik looked at me sideways. "It's just a hunch. Start now."

"It's going to be tough to follow him in a small town. He's going to spot the tail, if he's that smart. He'll be on us faster than a fat man at a buffet."

He was right, of course. "I see no option," I said.

I watched Whitman leave and get into his car. I half expected he would look back, or give himself a high five that he pulled it off. But no hint of anything. "You're hiding something," I muttered. Derik left right behind him.

I got some good news, sort of. When I got back to my desk, I checked my phone for a message. Someone was willing to buy Mom's house. At thirty five thousand below asking, with no conditions and an immediate possession. I told the agent to take it and I'd be over in the morning to sign the papers. With the economy on the verge of gong down the drain, I figured I'd better take it while the going was good. Besides, the nursing home was bugging me to make a payment.

Finally, my luck was starting to change. Maybe I'd find out what really happened to Easton. Maybe it would send me to homicide on Harrison Street.

Pam and I consoled each other over a dinner out on the town. Selling the house, which my parents owned for more than half a century, was the end of an era.

In the morning I was to head to Mom and tell her the news. I expected she would be depressed at losing her house. I was looking forward to the visit now that she was out of the coma, and back at the nursing residence, but I was a bit concerned about how she would take the news of her beloved home.

Sunday October 3rd

Pam and I spent the weekend going through Mom's house to clear it out. What a daunting task. This was the only time in my life I wish I had siblings to help with it all. People accumulate so much "stuff", crap and worthless nonsense, I first thought, over their lives. I was soon to find out more than one shocker as we rummaged through everything.

I was glad my life didn't include accumulating things I didn't need. But now I had inherited all of this, which had to be dealt with.

I called movers in for the big belongings. I didn't need the couches, three beds, kitchen table set, fridge, carpets, and such. They all went to the Goodwill. They were far too old and worn out to be worth trying to sell on line. I kept some of the bed sheets, blankets and pillows. Pam staying with me showed one can never have enough of them.

Most of the kitchen utensils, some so old I had no idea what they were for, went with the movers. Dry food would go to the food bank.

The few family photos I kept, of course. Pam said she wanted Mom's jewellery, which wasn't much: a few bracelets, watches, and necklaces. Dad's wedding band I kept.

But the surprise of my life, well, the first one, was in my mother's bedroom. Mom kept all of Dad's clothes. I'd been after her for a while to dispose of them. But she couldn't muster the courage. So I assigned Pam to sort through his stuff, while I went through Mom's clothes. Most of it would go with the Goodwill guys.

In the top sock drawer I found half a dozen bankbooks. I looked through each one. Only one was current. Last used just before she went to the home. $1,200 was in it. But the other five books totalled almost one hundred grand. Some hadn't been updated in a decade. But they all had a consistent amount of money put into them every month.

I was stunned. In the last few years, Mom was always so frugal. I figured what she got from my father was barely enough to live on. Many times I gave her money, or brought in food for her, because I was worried she didn't have enough at the end of the month.

I'd have to legally close out those bank accounts, which meant another visit to the lawyer. I put the bankbooks in my purse.

But it's what Pam discovered which floored the both of us. In his top sock drawer was an envelope. Inside were newspaper clippings of his arrests. Some had really nice pictures of him in uniform. He was such a handsome guy.

We read through each one. A sense of pride and admiration filled our thoughts. What a testament to aspire to. I wondered if I could become like him.

In the very bottom drawer, under some old clothes, were three small boxes. She opened them. One was a Purple Heart, one was a Bronze Star and one was a Viet Nam Service Medal.

I never even knew my father was in the military, let alone in Viet Nam. He never said a word about it. Under the medals was a photograph in a frame. Four very young men in uniform, raggedy at that too, not just the uniforms they had on, but themselves too. The photograph was a black and white, obviously taken on a hilltop with all kinds of military equipment around them. Jungle was barely visible in the distance behind the figures.

The men were all smiles, two with thumbs up. Each one had an arm around the one beside him. The one on the end was my father. Dad couldn't have been more than eighteen.

I turned the photo over. Their names were written on the back, along with the date: July 23, 1963. Beside the three other names, written in a different pen, were the dates of each death: January 7th, 1964, November 21st, 1965, and November 21st, 1965.

Tears welled in my eyes. Pam hugged me. This was a part of my father's history I never new existed. It must have been so traumatic for him that he never said anything about it.

Under some old pants in the same drawer, Pam pulled out a German Walther P38 handgun. She quickly handed it to me as gingerly as possible. I dropped the mag, it was empty. I racked the action, nothing came out. The gun was also very old. I looked carefully at the picture, and in it Dad had a sidearm. Same gun. A World War Two German pistol was in the Viet Nam war?

I also noticed Dad had sergeant stripes. They were just visible on the arm he had around his buddy.

Pam found a high school yearbook. 1962, Dad's last year there. We looked for his picture. Wasn't hard to find, he circled it. But so too were three other boys circled. I looked carefully at the military picture and the school pictures.

"Mom, it's the same guys."

I couldn't speak. My throat welled up.

We found more of the four of them together. In particular was a picture of a varsity football game Dad's team won. He was the team's captain, and the four of them were arm in arm, just like the 'Nam photo. The uniforms were different, and instead of guns, there was a football, but it was the same photo, including the same two guys with their thumbs up.

I had to wonder. The Purple Heart meant he was wounded. The Bronze Star meant he did something significant. Two of his friends died on the same day. Did something happen, which precipitated those deaths and the medals? I wondered if I could find out.

I never knew about this part of my father's life. I wished he was around to explain all this.

Lastly we tackled the basement. Boxes and boxes of stuff, mostly old clothes. Dad's workroom was left to the end. It was in with the furnace, and was a tortuous moment.

I didn't want the tools, and he had a lot of them. Jars of screws, bolts, nuts, nails—those went with the Goodwill guys.

My father was also into building model cars and trucks as a kid. He never built any when I knew him, but the ones he completed were always on one of these shelves, now with a coating of dust so thick their paint was obscured. There were about a dozen of them.

I carefully put them in a box to take home.

"Why are you keeping those?" Pam inquired.

"Something Dad did with his hands. Those I keep."

In the bench below those shelves were boxes upon boxes of unmade kits. Models Dad bought so long ago but never found the time to build. I pulled them out to put in boxes, which the movers took upstairs. But that exposed the biggest bombshell of all time.

Two metal boxes were under the kits. Both were locked. Pam and I looked around for the keys—dumping jars of screws, and such. But no luck.

We finally opened one with a screwdriver and hammer. Our hearts stopped. Immediately a musty smell emanated from the box. It was full of money.

The Goodwill guys were still emptying the basement, so we

closed the door to the room and giddily counted it. Most of it was $100 bills, and obviously very old. They were bundled together into $10,000 groups. There were twenty of those. Plus another fifty thousand in unbundled bills of various denominations.

"Where did Grandpa get all this?" Pam said, both excitedly, but also apprehensively.

I started to sweat as the amount sunk in.

"I have no idea. This is one fuck of a lot of money. No way he could have saved this, and what we saw in those bankbooks."

"You think he stole this, or got bought off?"

I didn't want to answer what I first thought of her jumping to that conclusion. How could she assume that? I got angry, but I realized what was unthinkable. She might be right.

"I don't know, Pam."

We sat on the floor, just looking at it. My Dad... The hero we just discovered upstairs... Was on the take.

"What do we do with it?" Pam said quietly, almost whispering.

Do I take it in? Hand it over, and destroy my father's image and reputation? I felt guilty that I would even contemplate keeping it. But to destroy my father's legacy on the force was inconceivable.

Pam picked up my thoughts.

"Makes you wonder what's in the other case, Mom. Open it."

Inside the other case were stock certificates. IBM, Bank of America, American Airlines, GE, some mining stocks, and other high quality corporate stocks. I'd have to check on their face value, but some of the stocks were issued in the 1970s.

However, many of them were from the entire 1950s decade. My grandfather did work as a senior aircraft designer for Grumman. Maybe some of these were past down to my father. But this still left me with some doubt as to where the rest came from.

"Mom, there could be a million dollars here."

It hit me like a truckload of newspapers. She was probably right, but also, it meant that, again, no way my father could have saved this on his cop salary. My mom had a few good jobs over the years, including being the floor manager at JC Penney's. But she lost that job when the store closed a decade or so ago.

Is it possible to have saved that much? No way, I thought.

I was trying to justify my denial.

A life my father had I never knew—no one knew. I wished he was around to explain all of *this*. Mom might know. Next visit I'd have to bring it up.

We closed the cases and taped them shut.

The movers were done when we emerged from the room.

"Mom, what if there were more secrets those guys took?"

We ran up the stairs, but by the time we got out the front door, the truck was far up the street. Too late now.

Finally by the end of the day, after I loaded up my car, stuffed more like it, the house was completely empty. In all my years I had never seen it empty. It was a sad sight. It was too much to take in all at once.

The two of us stopped sweeping, and cried.

Day 18, Wednesday October 6th

Derik called just as I was heading to court.

"Whitman gave me the slip."

"He what?" I said, stopping on the steps to the courthouse. "How the hell did he do that?"

"I don't know. He stopped at a mall here in Chicago. I went inside to follow him, but lost him in the crowd. So I went back to his car but it was gone. It couldn't have been a few minutes. He must know we're tailing him."

Fucker. He is guilty.

"Head back to his house and talk to some neighbours. He must have someone looking after his animals while he's gone. See if anyone knows what he's up to. I gotta go into court, but you get back to me the second you find him."

I got out of court late, well past dinnertime and I was starving, but not hearing from Derik, I had to call him.

"Hi Marg. I talked with the neighbours. One was asked to look after his animals for a few days. Seems Whitman leaves for two to three days every week. She said Whitman goes south of the lake to watch migrating birds this time of year."

Swell. "Ok, stay there and call me the instant Whitman gets back."

"You going to sign the voucher for my motel bill?"

"Fuck it, yes."

"Wonderful. I gotta call my wife, again, that I'll be gone for a couple days." He hung up.

Derik didn't believe me that Whitman had something to do with Easton's disappearance. But I just can't get it out of my mind. All this week we argued the possibilities. He was still convinced Easton was in Brazil with a woman. Absconding with money from the company.

We finally got the company investments, and there was nothing glaring. I wasn't expecting anything concrete about them for at least a couple weeks. The forensic accounting guys up stairs were swamped with cases.

I think he's dead, was in my mind a lot. I was expecting his body to float ashore any day. I still thought it could be Whitman. But I had no new evidence. His claim of being on some camping trip in Canada may or may not have been true. Problem was, the camp Whitman said he went to was closed this time of year. There was no way to verify he was there.

It wasn't just his lack of emotion. It was the phrase he used when he introduced me to the parrot in the cage. He said, "I don't cage my friends." Did he cage his enemies? He certainly hated Easton enough even today, after all those years.

I got home to find Pam all packed.

"What gives? You're moving out?"

"Yes, Mom. Thank you so much for helping me out. Angel and I are getting back together. He wants to marry me. But we have to move to Florida. He's got a new job with his uncle there. It's a good salary too."

"What about his infidelity?"

"He said I over reacted. He didn't do anything. They were just friends."

"And you believed him?"

"I have to, Mom, he's the father of my child. He wants this baby. He wants to start a family."

"When do you leave?"

"He's coming to pick me up in a few minutes. You'll get to finally meet him."

Sure enough, a Latino man came off the elevator. He smiled at Pam. She smiled back. He gingerly passed me to hug and kiss Pam.

"Mom, this is Angel. Angel, this is my mother."

"Pleasure to meet you Miss Cunningham, ma'am. Pam has talked a lot about you."

We shook hands. He seemed nice enough. Good looking fella too. We went into the apartment to have a chat.

They didn't stay long as they had to get going. Pam convinced me she was doing the right thing.

Pam pulled me aside when Angel left the apartment with some of her bags. "Come with us, Mom. Quit your job. You don't have to work any more, you know." She winked.

I chuckled. "We'll see. But here." I handed her a box. She opened it. In it were two bundles of the 100s, and a number of stock certificates. "That'll get you guys started. Buy a house, I hear they're now pretty cheap in some places."

"Don't stocks have to be transferred?"

"I'll sort those out with a lawyer later, you hold on to them in the mean time."

Pam smiled so much her face lit right up. She gave me a huge hug. Heading out the door she said, "Come live with us."

I shook my head a little. "I have a case I have to see through first. When I'm done, maybe."

Day 20, Friday October 8th

Derik called late afternoon. Whitman had come home. Derik talked with him, and Whitman claimed he was bird watching south of Lake Erie. He showed Derik the photos he took. When asked about the mall, losing the tail, Whitman claimed he didn't even know he was being tailed, and it was a quick decision to not go into the mall after all. He said he had turned around and walked back out.

Whitman was angry with Derik, asking why he was being tailed. Whitman asked when he was getting his computer back as we were costing him money, and his web clients were getting angry he was unable to make changes to their websites.

Forensics wasn't finished going through his machine. These things take a few weeks, especially with the backlog we had.

I got home late that evening to a message to call my Aunt May,

It was the most devastating call of my life. Mom had died. She tried to get out of bed and fell hitting her head on a chair. She was dead before they got her to the hospital.

I had to go to the morgue to identify her body. I also had to make all the funeral arrangements, and contact everyone Mom knew. With my daugher in Florida and my mother dead. I was all alone in the world.

I called the squad room and got three days bereavement.

The most paradoxical thought crossed my mind when I hung up the phone. With Mom now gone, so too was my father's secret.

Day 23, Wednesday October 13th

Because I had to deal with my mother, my weekly meeting with Chief David was postponed until the morning before the funeral. I was down to just three cases. David hadn't been assigning anything new to me the last couple weeks. He realized I was overloaded.

I explained where I was with the two easy ones, both completed with success. I left Easton's case for last.

"So, where are we on Easton?" David said looking at my report.

"Nothing new for more than a week."

"Is he dead or in Brazil?"

"I don't know."

"Well, it looks to me he's in Brazil, doesn't it?" he said.

"Maybe. The trail's an orgy of evidence though."

"You think it's too good to be true? You think most of this is false evidence?" he said cocking his head to the right.

"I do."

He paused to think. He sighed. Shaking his head a bit, "You know my brother's a geology professor at Tufts U, right? Well, he's an investigator of sorts. Uses evidence to try to piece together past events. Very past events, actually. Anyways, he always told me something about how to pick which of several competing theories best fits the evidence. The Rule of Parsimony."

I looked confused. I had no idea what that word even meant. Never heard it before.

"The Rule of Parsimony. The simplest explanation tends to be the correct one. Seems in your case the simplest explanation is Easton's gone rabbit with company coin and some dame."

He looked at me hard as he closed the folder.

"So, you're going to pass this on to the FBI right? Something you should have done three weeks ago."

"Fuck the FBI. This is my case. I'm not done yet, something's going to come up."

"No, you're done. This aint goin' anywhere."

"Ah, c'mon, Boss!"

"Look, Marg, you did the best you could," David said as he put my report down and sat back in his chair. "You're done with this case."

"Swell. But my gut feeling is this isn't over yet. The wife can't wait to get her husband's life insurance."

"And she won't get anything. We don't have a body and we aren't considering him for the no body club. As far as we're concerned he's alive. That's what I told her this morning."

"I'm not convinced. We haven't even gotten the bank transfer records from the Caymans yet."

"And you won't. I got a call from the police there. They won't investigate. They don't see anything illegal and as far as they're concerned it's private information. You've reached the end of the line, I'm afraid."

Swell. That feeling of helpless frustration is quite uncomfortable. "C'mon, Boss. Whitman definitely has an axe to grind. He even went to Easton's house to kill him. Twice he planned to kill him. He may have had something to do with Easton's disappearance."

"Do you have any evidence to back that up with?"

"No," I reluctantly admitted.

"Are you expecting a breakthrough any time soon?"

"No," I said, grudgingly. I ground my teeth in frustration.

"Then you're done with this case. Call off the surveillance, and give Whitman his computer back, today. He's called every day demanding we return his ability to make a living. I'm closing this case, right now. I'm passing this on to the FBI."

"Swell." My entire reason for being a cop just evaporated. My face filled with anger.

"Sorry, Marg, but that's from the top. Now, you've got no new cases. You're all cleaned up, right?"

"Affirm. So what's my next case?"

"None. You're taking two weeks off."

Time off? What the hell is "time off?" It's twiddling my thumbs in boredom and frustration, that's what time off means. Though, I will get to finish those two books. I was just about to say something.

"No objections. You've had no vacations, ever, that I can see in your file. You just lost your mother, your daughter's pregnant and moved to Florida. That reminds me, I haven't gotten a notice when your mother's funeral will be."

It took some effort, as my throat locked up in a quiver. "It's..." I took a breath, and let it out quickly, "it's tomorrow."

"Marg, you need to let everyone know. I, and many others, want to pay our respects. I never worked with your father. But a lot of guys here say he was a top-notch cop, straight, fair and honest. They miss him at homicide."

I smiled a little, especially at the irony and said, "Thanks, David, that means a lot. Mom's going to be buried beside him."

"Well, even more reason to have everyone at the precinct there. We can give a salute to your ol' man at the same time. After the funeral, take some time off and go be with your daughter. That's an order. Now get out of here and enjoy yourself for a change."

It was right then I realized my father's secret had to be protected.

"Guess this means any promotion to homicide is out."

"I put your paper work in, with a glowing recommendation. It's out of my hands now."

As I headed to the door, I stopped and turned to David. "With what's going on in the world, I just may stay in Florida."

"You'll be greatly missed if you choose to do that."

"Swell, but some how I highly doubt it."

I left the room.

PART 3

I kept two steps ahead

I had just sat down for lunch, opened a can of Coke with an old episode of the original Star Trek coming on, the one on the Doomsday Machine, and about to take a bite when the phone rang.

Why is it that the fucking phone rings right when you start something? Are people at the other end clairvoyant? Fucking phone is an intrusion into my privacy.

Ring two, and I was looking around the couch in vane for the portable.

Ring three, gawdamnit I have to get up and get it in the kitchen.

Ring four: "Hello."

"Mister Whitman?"

"Yes".

"This is detective Marg Cunningham of the Chicago Police Department."

And now it starts. Time for the performance of all time.

"Ok. And you are calling me for what?"

"You were fired from Insur-Data in two thousand and one, correct?"

"Shit, I hadn't thought about that in years, and now you bring it up. Thanks for spoiling my lunch." I made sure I sounded angry.

Almost convinced myself.

"I need to ask you some questions."

"About what? What can I possibly tell you about that slimeball?"

"Sir, your name came up in our investigation. So, either I come and pay you a visit, or I will make sure you come down here and visit us in our interrogation room. Take your pick.'

"When? I was just about to sit down for lunch."

"Today, I can drive up now."

"Hmmm. What's this actually about?" I gotta sound like there is nothing from me.

"We don't discuss cases over the phone."

"Well, I'm not going to agree to a blind date unless I know something as to why I should agree. I haven't had any dealings with that shitbag in ten years. I have nothing to share."

"I need to be thorough."

Oh, she's good. Hard to turn her down.

"It will be a short visit. Four hours of driving you know. On the city's dime, not mine."

"I guess I have no real choice do I?" I didn't want to sound too defensive for the visit. I fully expected this.

"Nope."

"Fine."

"I'm on my way." She hung up.

Guess I'd better clean up a bit first. Gawdamnit, missed the first part of my show. I did finish my lunch first.

By the time the second Star Trek ended (it was a marathon that day on the Space Channel), and I posted a few Tweets, there was only thirty minutes to do a bit of clean up. Not possible with two parrots, and an English Mastiff. My companions were a cockatoo and a Timmy African Grey. I have a large cage at the front window for them to look out side, but I never close the door.

I don't cage my friends, only my enemies.

Rug, that's the dog's name, is just that. Like me he doesn't like to expend too much energy doing things.

I don't live in a museum. Certainly living alone helps, no one on your case to keep things tidy.

I figured the kitchen is where we should sit. Better clean the dishes off the table at least. Maybe I should put some pots from the stove into the sink and load the dishwasher.

Didn't get too far when I saw the car drive up.

Not pretty, but an attractive women. Hansom I guess is the proper word. Kinda reminded me of Trinity a bit. I like those types. They aren't shallow and vain about themselves. She looks late thirties, maybe late forties, I would guess. She has short black hair. She's a tall thin build. No ring on "the" finger. Workaholic likely. That could be a problem. But I have rehearsed this several times in the past two weeks. So my story should be rock solid. We are about to find out.

I answered the door before she knocked. I introduced her to my companions. She also asked about my father's medals on the wall, how he got them.

"My father was with Patton at Kaserine Pass, where he got his first Purple Heart," I said with pride. "He got back with his unit in Sicily where he got his second Purple Heart and the DSC. He got the Silver Star and the third Purple Heart when he was involved with rescuing Patton's son from a POW camp. That flag..." Now my throat started to choke. "My father rose that flag in a German town after Patton crossed the Rhine. Apparently, my father was part of a group that found a concentration camp full of Gypsies and Jews. That, my father said, was the worse time in the whole war for him.

"They found some of the German guards pretending to be inmates. But clearly they were too well fed. My father lined them up against a wall and personally shot every one of the dozen or so with that very rifle.

"After he shot the Germans, my father went into the town near by, arrested the Mayor, pulled down the Nazi flag, and erected that flag there on the town hall."

Even explaining this to a stranger brought tears to my eyes.

"After the war, when my father was part of the occupying force in Germany, he was almost court marshalled for that shooting at the camp. His lieutenant complained saying my father disobeyed an order to not execute the Germans. They were prisoners of war and should be tried in a court. Patton personally intervened to stop the court marshal.

"I can't imagine what it would have been like back then. My father was a true American hero. He did what was right to do."

Unmoved by my explanation, the cop looked around the living room, then the dining room where my computer was, and ended in the kitchen.

We sat at the table across from each other. This is when the cops look for body language. I gotta make sure I was poker faced the whole time. No emotions at all. Of course, the first question is always the first question from a cop.

"Where were you on September the tenth?"

"Wait. I don't understand. Why are you asking me about a specific date? What's shithead got to do about that date?"

"Mr. Whitman, I ask the questions," she retorted. "So, where were you on September the tenth?"

Time for my air tight alibi.

"I was in the mountains around Kamloops."

"In Canada?"

"There's no other Kamloops."

"How long were you there?"

"Two weeks, I came home yesterday."

"You have proof?"

"I flew American Airlines from O'Hare to Vancouver. I didn't stay at any hotels, I camped in the mountains."

"You went camping in September?"

"Best time, few people. I prefer fewer people."

"When did you leave?"

"The eighth—no the seventh." Gotta have some things that I wouldn't get right.

She wrote all this down. "What did you do with your animals?"

Weird question, why does she care? Obviously, I found a place for them.

"Obviously I sent them away for the two weeks. My wife took Rug, and I belong to a parrot group, and we look after each other's birds when we have to leave."

Alibi set.

We went over my time at the company, how without my expertise Easton would never have gotten off the ground. How he pressured me to leave the State and work for him full time. As well as the promise of permanent work. Then we came to my firing.

"Yes," I said. "And I sued his ass. Didn't get what I wanted, but the judge did give me a good settlement. Drove Fuckhead up the wall. He stormed out of the courtroom."

"You sued Easton for wrongful dismissal?" she said.

"No, breach of contract. But the only way he could fire me was to frame me for a mistake I didn't do."

"Their records said you screwed up a client's project. Something about misinformation in the data and wrong analysis."

"Liars. It was a set up."

"You know that for a fact?"

"Yes. I knew the data. I knew how it was set up, how much data that was entered, and how it was analysed. I had completely automated the analysis process. My coding would fire the Stored Procedures, dump the recordsets into Excel, and then add the appropriate type of equations depending upon the data type."

She was writing this all down.

I explained that there was no new data, but he wanted a new run. I explained in detail how the data was screwed up, but not by me. That's when the shit happened, and he fired me on the spot. He broke his word about employment with him.

"So, I sued. He did promise me employment for life. Did his father tell you that?"

"His father? What does his father have to do with anything?"

"Any investigator worth their value would have already

interviewed people at the company before now. So, I assume you talked with his father about me." I said. I paused a bit, as if making an after thought. "And what is it exactly you are investigating? Did Shithead finally get caught doing something illegal?"

"No, he never said anything about you. But I did see that in the court transcript. You made the case and won. You clearly retired early from the State to work for them."

"I had evidence I presented. It won the case."

"Saw that. Pretty clear to me. So, you were angry."

"Fucking right I was."

She paused a bit writing in her pad. Then she tried to side track me with personal questions.

"You married, Mr. Whitman?"

I showed her the ring. "I am, but separated."

"When did you get separated?"

I explained that I couldn't get a job. That we lost our home, the place where we raised our family. And how my wife left me because of my depression.

"You threaten Mr. Easton?"

"Yes, with the lawsuit."

"No, I mean verbally threaten him."

That wasn't my style, I explained.

"Wanted to kill him?"

And there was the question. I leaned forward, looked her sternly in the eyes. "Damn straight I did. I wasn't the only one. So he's missing, that's what your investigating isn't it."

"I never said he was missing."

That came quick.

"Why else would you ask if I wanted to kill him? Have you found his body?" I asked her.

She was silent for a few seconds, then said, "No crime wanting to kill someone."

Damn straight it's no crime to want someone dead. Just the act is.

Can't let that out, though. She continued.

"Yes, I noticed he has a long list of people let go. Big turnover. So, you wouldn't be unhappy if he disappeared?"

Marg was clearly paving the road for me to tell her who Easton was.

"What do you mean by disappeared? You didn't answer my question, so I suspect you haven't found his body. Maybe he's run off with company money."

"What makes you think he's done something illegal?"

"From you. If he's not dead, but missing, then why else would you be investigating Shithead?

"I never said anything as to why I was investigating. He could be dead for all I know."

Oh, man could I mind fuck her right now. But I had to sow the seeds of my plan in her mind. I need to look and act confused.

"I'm confused then. Why would he be dead?" I said. "Did someone finally put him out of our misery? Wouldn't surprise me. Do you want to know the real reason why he fired me?"

"Something not in the court transcript?"

"Oh, yeah, because I had no evidence. Just a huge hunch."

"Share it."

"He's a womanizer. Loves to have just women working for him. Just before my incident with him, which caused my firing, he had a woman come and evaluate the efficiency of his employees." I explained that this woman Easton hired checked everything in the company, including my software. "I suspect Easton replaced me with her and set me up so she could get my job."

Marg queried me as to why he would deliberately set me up.

Nothing in my explanation was a lie, but I needed to frame the next part carefully to lead Marg down the road I wanted. It needed to plant in her mind that Easton had taken off with someone.

"I havn't been there in ten years, but knowing Easton I suspect he has not changed. What is the ratio of female employees to male employees?"

She sat there silent for a second looking down at the table. Then looked up at me. "He has only one male employee, the rest are women."

"Of course. Did you notice one thing all those women have in common?"

"Other than being female, they are competent? Maybe, just maybe, he happens to have competent women employees."

"If only that were true. The one thing they all have in common is they all have big tits. Easton is a tit man. He loves to surround himself with large tits." Marg looked uncomfortable. She doesn't believe me. But this was all true. Actually, I was quite disgusted with Easton for this. I continued, "Every male person he had working for him, within a year, he replaced them with a woman with big tits. I think he took his inspiration from Charlie Wilson."

I wondered if she knew who Wilson was. I'm sure she will check.

"I hadn't noticed. Who interviewed you?" she said ready to write a name in the pad.

"I don't remember her name. But I do remember she was tall and liked to show her well formed cleavage."

I got another stare. Then looking down at her pad she said, "She still works there, she's their IT manager, your job."

"I fucking knew it!" Of course, I already knew that. I'd been spying on the prick for months preparing my plan. I'd seen him with her in his office, and not just for work related issues.

On one of the evenings I was across the road spying to lay out my plan. I could see the two of them through the large window to his office. I watched as he undressed her, completely topless. Then they both disappeared below the window. They didn't surface for several minutes.

"I'm going to have to be frank with you, Mr. Whitman," she said sternly. "You sound fucking sexist to me. How do you know he is a breast man?"

I explained about the day I found him with several new female employees on the floor. He could look right down their tops. It really bothered me after I realized what he was doing. I contemplated talking to the women about it. They too must have been uncomfortable. When does a boss get female employees on the floor? But I lost my nerve. I regret not doing anything about that. I protected my ass instead of defending the dignity of the woman working for the shithead. One of the reasons I had to lock him up.

"That does sound strange," she said finishing note taking.

"I also found pornography on his computer," I said. I explained how I had to work on his personal machines when he wasn't around, to update things, and such. I told her I found all kinds of porno files on his laptop. Marg paused a few times in her writing as I hit some juicy parts.

"Hmm, I have to admit, this is a new side of Easton."

She wrote more notes. None of this was a fabrication. It indeed is what I found.

"But there's more," I said.

"More, how much more could there be?"

"He had had affairs with several of the woman on staff. He also had affairs with women when he want on trips to various events around the country."

That made her look up at me. "You know this for a fact?"

"Yes. I almost caught him and his personal secretary coming out of the woman's washroom. He forgot to zip his fly."

"Who was that?"

Rug came in at that point, and flopped himself at Marg's feet. She seemed to like him. She reached down and scratched behind his ears. He really liked it when people did that. When she stopped, Rug looked up as if to say "that's all, WTF?" His eyes were so full of expression.

"Sorry, I'm real bad with names. Just check who it was with his records when I was there. She came on board about two years before I left."

Oh, yeah. She is gobbling all this up. I can tell by the way she is concentrating writing this down, I've got something new for her. None of this was fiction. Thus, when she checks into this she was going to get an eyeful.

I continued, "I went on one trip. The one and only time. He used me as a showcase. When I explained how our methodology worked, it would woo the client. I went to many meetings in Chicago, but only one outside the city. That was Washington, DC. It was a convention of small insurance companies and we were meeting with half a dozen potential clients."

I explained the gorgeous woman from one of the companies we met with was eyeing him. The two of them took off together that night. Again, I was so disgusted with his behaviour; I never again went on another trip with him. I found some excuse not to go. He wasn't happy with me. He needed me to be his shadow for wooing the client. He would use our programming terminology to make himself sound authoritative and knowledgeable. With his "IT Manager" present it added to the authority when he spoke like that. Actually, he was using these terms in completely the wrong context. I never corrected him. I regret that too.

One day he took me out to lunch after a meeting with a client. He wanted to celebrate them signing the contract. He took me to a strip bar by the airport. The girls were totally naked, provocatively dancing on the stage. Now, I like the female form, no question. My wife and I would have great days naked together once we got the kids off to school. But this was not what I want to do with someone. I sat with my back mostly to the stage, eating my burger as fast as I could. He was glued to the bouncing boobs. One of his expressions forced me to turn and look. She was facing away, bent over with her ass and all in our direction, looking back at us from between her legs. It was barely two meters away. She was clearly egging him on.

Easton got up and placed a C note on the stage for her. She could see it looking down between her spread legs. I half expected him to stuff it in her vagina. But he didn't. I was still disgusted.

Hey, my wife and I were great together sexually. I loved it when she would pose for me in such fashions. But that was between two people who loved each other, and enjoyed making pleasure with each other.

I had to wonder, as we were heading back to the office, if he had the loving wife I did. I didn't need the extra-marital excitement. Obviously he did.

When I got home that night, being met by my love, I felt I betrayed my wife. I explained it all to her. She actually asked me that maybe I had made a mistake working for him.

I found excuses to not have lunch with him again.

"So, if I were you, if he has taken off, I'd look at who he had been with lately," I said. "He's likely taken off with someone. His wife is a real bitch, you know. She used to hound him all the time about not making enough money. I figured he'd leave her one day. You're looking for him—that's what this is about isn't it?"

That was the dig I needed to set. Laid the groundwork for my fantasy. Well, not really a fantasy. This was all true. It's as if Easton set the plan up for me.

"I will take that under advisement. Did Easton know anyone from Brazil?"

There it is, Brazil. They're following my trail all right. The aim was now away from me. Now I just had to give her part two to slam-dunk the case to ignore me. But I also can't give any hint I knew about this.

"So, he *is* missing. Interesting." I paused getting repositioned. "Not that I know of; his business was only in the US. Though in my last year he was looking to get business in Europe and Mexico. So by now he could have expanded to Brazil, it's a fast growing economy.

"However, there's more that could have impact on his missing."

"There is more?" she asked looking up from her pad.

"Have you checked into the company's books?"

"None of your business," she said sternly.

"Do you know he has a shadow company with a silent partner? He was using that shadow company to buy homes around the university and then renting them out to students."

She was writing more down.

"That's not illegal," she said not looking me.

"No, but sending fake invoices to Insur-data for services not rendered is."

She stopped writing and looked me straight in the eyes. "You have proof of this?"

She was catching on quickly.

"Absolutely I did. On one of those computer update days, when no one was there, a Saturday if I remember, I had to update Windows on his machine. I accidentally double clicked on the Excel icon on the desktop. It opened blank, but you know under files where the last spreadsheets are listed?"

She nodded while writing.

"One of them was this shadow company. I opened it."

"That was illegal," she said.

"Then arrest me. Do you want to know what I saw or not?" I was genuinely sarcastic.

She paused the writing and just looked down at the pad. "What the fuck, go ahead." She returned to writing again.

"He has billed, on a regular monthly basis, his own company for a total of some one million."

She stopped writing and with eyes wide open she asked, "And tell me you copied and kept a copy of that file."

"No, at the time it was none of my business."

That was a lie. In fact, I did copy the file onto the main server, which I then emailed to myself, not from Outlook, as that leaves a trail. I wrote a quick program in Visual Basic and emailed it from there. No trace on the server. Not only that. I also wrote a program, which I planted on his machine, which copied that file to the server any time it got saved, and in turn was emailed to my home, then deleting the file off the server.

I had everything. Even the bank account number and password. And no, the idiot didn't even password protect the file. So I could log into his account any time I wanted. By the time I implemented my plan against him, the account had accumulated to three million.

"Do you have any more?" she asked.

"Not that I can think of off the top. It has been ten years, likely much has changed since I was forced out."

"OK, so I want to thank you for your time and information. It was most helpful after all wasn't it?"

"Well, good luck finding the prick. I hope he has done something really stupid and you lock his ass up for a long, long time.

"We'll find where he is," Marg said standing up.

I added, "Not if he's in Brazil. I suspect, maybe I'm wrong, but I'd bet the US has no extradition treaty with Brazil. If he's gone there. That's why you asked about it."

She drank the last of the glass of water and looked around the room. "I'm going to take this back to the office and see what I can find out. Thank you for your time. Should you remember more me please call me." She handed me her card. "Nice parrots by the way."

She had to carefully step over Rug, who didn't acknowledge her move, he just grunted and snorted.

"Definitely not a guard dog," she said.

"No, we don't need guard dogs here. We have no crime at all. No one locks their doors here. This is a really nice neighbourhood."

She left. I looked at my Dad's photo. Second battle won, but the war continues. "I pulled it off!" I said aloud. She was on the trail I had painted for her. Like Hansel and Gretel following breadcrumbs. She was going to conclude that Easton absconded with the three million with someone he had recently met. I could rest easy, or so I thought.

I had to make another food delivery to Easton in the morning. Just had to make sure Marg hadn't put a tail on me. Though, she really had no reason to assume I had anything to do with his disappearance.

I couldn't wait too long, the sun was going to set soon. So I had to make my check on Easton quick. I logged into a client's computer using Remote Desktop, typed in the IP address, waited a few seconds, and there he was.

I had installed a small web-cam in the far corner of the room he was in. He wouldn't be able to see it tucked up in the ceiling. As normal, he was just sitting on the edge of the bed, staring ahead, like in a trance. Mice were scurrying around his feet.

Tomorrow I had to head to the barn to drop his next week of food. I carefully calculated the bare minimum calorie requirement.

In the morning, I arranged for my animals to be looked after, like I do every weekend. I then drove three hours south west of Chicago. I turned on a dead end dirt road well off the beaten track. Only three farms were on this road, one farm had no home, just the land rented for crops, and the other at the end of the road was a horse farm owned by a retired couple. Thus, traffic on the road was nearly none at all.

The property the barn was on actually belonged to Vicky, my wife – well, former wife. It was her parents' and in their family for generations. We used to go up there a lot when we were first married and her parents were still alive. The plan was for us to retire there. That was never going to happen. She never went back after her parents died. But she couldn't make herself sell the place. She wanted to pass it down.

The farm was almost two hundred acres, but only sixty was cleared, the rest, beyond a small creek, was all bush. The barn was made in the late 1800s from the timber on the property. It had been in the family that long. Vicky's brothers and father used to deer hunt on the property every fall. They hadn't done that since her father died some decade before. Hence, it was very quiet, and isolated.

Now that Vicky's parents were gone there was no one there to look after the property. The old house needed to be torn down anyway. Vicky's father, in his last years before dementia took over, just let the house go into ruin. The barn, though it needed repairs, was holding up quite well. It used to be a horse barn as the old guy used to breed and sell horses.

The barn had two levels, the upper level had stalls, so too did the lower level. Easton was in one of the lower level stalls.

I got there just after dark. I made sure I parked the car near the house, so he couldn't hear it come up the drive. I expected he'd be sleeping anyway, that late at night.

I got things ready in the house first, then around midnight I headed into the barn and set up his food.

Before I gave him the food, I had to make sure the batteries for the video link were fully charged by swapping them out with fresh units. He was usually woken up by me sending the food through the iron door, so I do that last, and in total darkness.

The drop today was the usual, a loaf of whole wheat bread, one jar of peanut butter, one jar of strawberry jam, and today a treat, a six-inch length of klobassa meat.

I spent the night in the old house and headed back home in the morning.

Like every morning, the first thing I did after letting Rug out was to cross out a day on the calendar, which I hid before Marg showed up. I stroked out September 28th, day nineteen. I fed my birds, then myself, then got on the computer and checked on my only caged animal.

He was inserting a length of straw into the wall. He was trying to count the days. He ate a bit of bread, pasting it with some jam and peanut butter with his fingers. The phone rang, I logged out.

Vicky called in a panic. There was always the unexpected. Marg, the cop, interviewed my wife. Holy fuck! That I was not expecting.

Vicky left me about two years after I got fired, just before I won my case against Easton. She just could not take my depression. She couldn't handle that I didn't want to work for anyone again. Sure, I did a bit of web programming, part time, here and there. Nothing steady. Provided me with a bit more money. But Vicky worked hard, more than full time at the TV station. She was a producer for children's shows. That meant long hours. Consequently, we saw little of each other.

Our only child was grown up and employed in her career off in San Francisco. She was to get married next year. Eight years prior, Vicky had had enough of my depression, it was affecting her work, and we split. That's when I moved out of Chicago and into my father's home, living with him until he died. He willed me the house.

Vicky comes to visit only once or twice a year. We see each other at Christmas and Thanksgiving with our daughter, but that's about it. No, when I went to Canada for my visits, Vicky didn't take Rug. I left him at a kennel on a nearby farm. He loved it there, lots of other dogs, all smaller than him.

I did't get out much. My interaction with people was mostly virtual through Yahoo Groups, Twitter and Facebook. I prefered that. My experience with Easton had taught me that people are untrustworthy, selfish pricks. You really see that online, when not eye-to-eye, people say what they really feel. People are pathetic myth believers. They *ad hominen* attack at the drop of a hat. People deep down are pathetic, especially those on the left of the political spectrum. The fewer people I personally meet with the better. My pet companions were far more honest than the vast majority of people I knew or had met only online. Sometimes I did't even know why I bothered to be online.

I was never like that before my experience with Easton. In fact, I was popular at high school. I joined the National Guard while I was at university; to not only get a little extra money, but also the camaraderie. I had a lot of fun with people in those days. But Easton smashed any of that I had left. I'd become almost a hermit.

"I had a call from a police detective yesterday," she said. "Ed, what have you done?"

"What did you tell her?"

"What do you think? I told her you wanted to kill Easton and bought a gun and almost carried it out."

Oh, fuck. Holy fuck. She told the cop that?

I had to tell Vicky about this when I wanted to execute Easton. It was eating me up inside. I had no one I could confide to. I could never keep secrets from her. She was my soul mate, through and through. Still is.

"Why would you do that?" I said. "They're going to suspect me in his disappearance now."

"Because I'm concerned. Did you do something you shouldn't have?"

Shit. I have never lied to my wife. Of all the fights we had I respected her too much to lie. Besides, she knew a lie. But I had no choice. This time I had to protect her for the same reason I didn't carry out the execution those many years ago.

"No, nothing." That hurt to say. "They think he took off with someone, with money he stole from the company."

"The cop didn't tell me that."

"No, she wouldn't. What else did you tell her?"

"Only that you needed help. It's not healthy for you to be squirreled away in that house and not going anywhere, not doing anything."

"I'm fine. Nothing to worry about."

"That's a lie."

As I said.

Ok, so that meant the cop was going to come back. Guaranteed. That also meant they would search my house. So what I need to do was to burn that calendar. Luckily, I had thought ahead to some extent. I'd get into a client's webserver through Remote Desktop so I could view the webcam in Easton's cell, hence no way the cops could trace that. Nothing was on my computer. I couldn't risk being found.

I had to make my next food delivery to Easton. It wasn't time yet for him to make his decision. He needed to suffer more first. Two more months at least. Thus, if they put a tail on me I've got to be able to shake them. That wasn't going to be easy.

Sure enough, two days later, a bit longer than I had expected, Marg called for another interview. I had only gotten back from last night's food drop a few hours earlier. She was very pushy. I had no choice. I had the place cleaned up a bit better this time. I got all the dishes done, a week's worth, and even cleaned the counters. Hell, I even shaved, something I do only once a week. But Marg called back and demanded I go to their precinct. Fuck. That's not good.

Her partner put me in the room as soon as I arrived. I looked around. It was a typical bland interrogation room. The grey paint was pealing off the block walls. The drop ceiling panels were stained with decades of cigarette smoke. A single stainless steel table was bolted to the middle of the floor. Two chairs were on either side of the table. Much like one sees on TV. A video camera was at the top right of the plate glass two-way mirror, which was beside the grey steel door. There was no light switch, nor any wall receptacles.

Of course, they were behind the glass. I gave a quick glance, as if I could see them.

Of course, they made me sweat it out for a couple hours before Marg came in. I sat in the chair, arms folded and appearing to be sleeping.

I slowly opened my eyes and raised my head when she finally came in. She slid a can of coke towards me. My favourite, she must have seen that when she was at my place. But this is how they get fingerprints. "No thanks. Trying to cut back."

She got right into the first question before she even sat down.

"Your wife says you tried to kill Easton. Want to tell me about this?"

She was pretty formal in the question. No hint of being angry, or trying to be my best buddy in hopes I open up to her. The weak ones fall for that stuff and spill their confessions without much effort.

I had no choice, however. I had to tell her the truth. But had to make sure it didn't lead her to consider me a suspect. Otherwise Easton would starve to death without ever knowing why. He needed another eight weeks before I could confront him with his choice. I had to perform better than an Oscar winner. I pretended to be surprised. Moving back in the seat with crossed arms is a defensive posture. Need to play the part.

"I was depressed. Big time. I couldn't find work. No one wanted to hire an over fifty, worn out, programmer when they could higher young people fresh with new skills. I'd have to go back to school and learn all the new stuff. Software changes fucking faster than light, and ten years at Insur-data got me out of sync with new stuff. I was too old to spend years learning all the Dot-Net syntax. So I was out of work and I saw no future for myself."

None of that was a lie. It destroyed my self-esteem, my worth to myself, and my family. I lost all confidence.

"Easton was evil—"

"Was?" she cut me off.

"Was, is, what's the difference? He used people for his own pleasure and goals, which was to get rich. He was clearly of the school 'the end justifies the end means.' I got it in my head to put a bullet in his brain.

"I went on the street and bought a Glock. I drove right in front of his home late at night. I was going to ring his bell and when he opened the door make his brains spatter on his perfectly clean floor."

"But you didn't follow through. Why not?"

I told her I prided myself on being logical. On being rational before I act. To plan things out before I act. I also had to make it appear to be poor me. I had to play the sympathy card about not being able to find work. It was true, of course, but I had to make it sound bad. Easy to do, because it was bad.

That night, with the gun in my hand, I sat there, in the dark, in the silence, thinking. How would I pull it off? Blast him in the head as he answered the door? Or wait until the morning and pop him as he backed up from the garage?

Killing someone is not me. Killing anything isn't me. I abhor hunting. I used to donate to animal rights groups, before Shithead fired me. I love all life. All life has the right to live free. That's why my pets aren't my pets, they're my friends, my companions. Especially now that I was alone in the world.

Pulling a trigger and executing someone was vile to my being. War was the only exception to that rule. Killing in war is the necessary evil to stop more killing. But I was so engulfed in rage, and contempt for the man that it fogged my rationality. I was at war with Easton. Someone had to put a stop to him, somehow, before he ruined more lives. Someone had to put an end to his charade of a life. That someone had to be me. But how? At the time I had no solution, no answer, no counter. I had to think of a better way.

"So I went to the harbour, and threw the handgun into the lake. Then I went home."

She didn't look up, just scribbled into her notebook.

I waited. She said nothing, just wrote.

What happened next would make or break my cover. I was getting a little nervous. But cops can spot that. I can't let anything expose me. *Poker face. Poker face. Control your emotions.*

She looked up at me. "What if the maid had answered the door instead of Easton? How would that have gone down with you standing at the door with a gun?"

Of course, the maid would have answered the door. One plan was to barge in, and hunt the fucker down in his house. I needed to act confused, as if I hadn't thought about that. Of course, I did. I sat in front of his house for hours, how can one not think about possible scenarios? So I played the part. "Wow, you know, I never even contemplated that. Shit, that's likely what would have happened. I just assumed he would have answered the door. Not sure what I would have done in that case, I hadn't thought about that."

"And what about the kids in the house? He had two at that time."

"Yeah, I did think about that. He usually doesn't allow them to be upstairs unless it's for dinner. I guess you saw they have all their toys in the basement. But back then one would have been a newborn, you're right."

"Would you have killed the whole family?"

Of course I wouldn't have. That would be mass murder of innocent people, and children. Easton wasn't innocent. He needed to be punished. He needed to be stopped from ruining more lives.

The rest of the family was a problem I would have had to deal with at the time. It was one of the reasons why I called the execution off. The kids. He had two at the time, a newborn and a four year old. If Easton and his wife tried to stop me, it could have turned out real ugly. Especially if the cops came before I could finish the job. I had resigned myself to suicide after killing him. But I wasn't going to go down as a mass—

"But they all would have been traumatized," Marg said cutting off my thought.

"Yes, just like Shithead traumatized the families of the people he fired. One guy killed himself, you know. Walked in front of a train.

I liked him, he was a good hardworking guy. So sad for his family. But to Fucknuts, that was just collateral damage. He knew about it. Fucker. They'd get over it, I heard him say. He said that about all those he fired."

"Would his family gotten over you murdering their father?"

"I'm not sure the wife's grief would have lasted too long, not once she got his life insurance and moved on."

She looked sternly at my eyes. "And that's when you got therapy?"

"Vicky told you about that too?"

Therapy… What crap. It's for weak-minded people who can't handle reality. I think those shrinks get off on making people ball their eyes out. They're sadists pretending to help people.

"Yes, amongst other things."

Of course, Vicky told her everything, that's Vicky. "Like what?"

"I ask questions here. How did the sessions go? Did they help your rage?"

No need to lie here. They didn't help me one bit. They guy always wanted to get into my past, confront me with bad things I've done in my childhood. He wanted to know my relationship with my father and my mother.

They so much want us to spill into a sobbing wreck about past events. As if unloading that weight helps people. Those sessions reminded me of the one scene in the Star Trek movie, The Final Frontier. The pains, because of our past mistakes, is who we are. It can't be cured, and shouldn't be cured. We aren't robots. We need our pain.

Besides, how the fuck did any of that past have to do with my anger because of Easton? Those six sessions were a total waste of my time. So I admitted the reality that they didn't help. It would be the best offensive move anyway.

"In a way yes. The sessions themselves didn't. Psychiatry is hocus pocus nonsense. The guy was OK, nice enough young fellow. But after six sessions that were costing me a fortune, I figured out that he wasn't helping me at all. I had to help myself. I had to let the Shithead go.

"So I did. It took a long time, but I eventually got to the point where I would remember him once a month, not every day. Eventually few things would remind me of those events. Until you called, that is. Now you have brought I back up again. It's going to take me months all over again. I thank you."

She could definitely see the knives thrusting from my eyes. Oscar on the way. Actually, I wasn't acting. I definitely was pissed off with her coming back a second time. Not my wife's fault. She's just too honest. Can't fault her for that. I should have planned better for that possibility. But I think I'm going to be OK.

Still writing she said, "Want to tell me about the radio controlled airplane?" She looked up into my eyes, waiting for an emotional response.

Fuck me. Vicky told her about that too. Shit, she didn't tell me that on the phone. But, of course, she would have told Marg. Luckily I'm a quick thinker, keep the poker face, turn it around.

"Yeah, another moment of lucid loss."

"For a whole year? OK. So tell me about it."

"Whatever my wife said, she always tells the truth."

That won't wash, she'll be looking for difference in our testimony.

"I need to hear it from you. All of it. Don't leave anything out."

I had no choice, but again I should be able to deflect this. Just tell the truth. "I spent a year on that. I made the barrel out of aluminium, because of the weight; you know a steel barrel is a tad heavy. However, you can only fire one round through an aluminium barrel. It destroys the rifling, and you can't use it again for a precision shot. So I made several of them for testing. It also put a six-power rifle scope on top of the barrel. To keep the friction down in flight, I placed the barrel pointing backwards, out the back of the plane.

"I modified one of those drone kits. They're pretty quick. I made it so the battery would be charged from solar panels on the body. The plane was going to be controlled through a cellphone by me on my computer with software I wrote. I even had a live video feed from the plane so I could fly it from my home as well as sight down the scope. Two video feeds, I mean.

"The idea was to fly the plane the night before onto the roof of the building across the road. Then wait until the end of the following day. Using the second video feed, I would be able to line the back of the plane and place the crosshairs on him, likely while he was on the phone. He'd be the most stable at that point. The distance I figured by using Google Earth was about 150 yards, simple enough shot to make.

"Once he'd been shot – I only had one chance at this – I would simply fly the plane off the roof. Then fly it out over Lake Michigan, where I'd crash it into the water tens of miles off shore. Hence, nothing would be found by you guys. It would be a big mystery.

"This method of executing him would offer one advantage over a direct shooting in the head like my first attempt. My family would never be embarrassed by me being caught, because there'd be no way you could catch me. There'd be no link between the shooting and me."

I continued to explain as Marg wrote everything down.

"The cops would have no way of knowing who or how the execution took place. It would be the perfect execution with no trace. Lots of questions, but no evidence. Sure the cops would figure out where the shot came from, but with no empty casing, and nothing on the roof, there would be nothing but mystery. There won't even be any witnesses of anyone getting on the roof, a three story ladder would be needed for someone to gain access to the roof. Hard to hide that. So the plan was perfect.

"The disadvantage was the Shithead would not know why. He would just cease to exist. It would also mean that his stuck up artificial wife would get his insurance, which would be substantial."

"Why didn't you carry it out if the plan was so perfect?" she asked not looking at me.

"Technical difficulties actually stopped the project and I abandoned it. The biggest problem was zeroing the scope to the barrel. No way to do that accurately. Besides, the big disadvantage was Shithead wouldn't know why. If I wanted to kill him, he needed to know it was me and why before hand. That would be critical in my opinion."

I finished with, "I eventually had to give it up. It was a great plan, but practically there were too many problems I kept running into, so I abandoned it. After that, I gave up wanting to kill him. I figured one day he'd get his comeuppance. Maybe he has.

"Besides, his artificial wife would get his insurance. You do know that's likely substantial."

One of my digs I needed to keep getting in, but I didn't think it registered.

The detective asked if I had anything left from the experiments. I told her I took a boat out onto the lake and sank it all at the bottom of the Michigan, including the computer I wrote the software on.

She then accused me of not wanting to leave a trail, implying I was guilty of his current situation.

She wrote everything down. "This is all before getting help, right?"

"Yes, my wife thought I was getting just a little obsessed. So she forced me to get help. You already know about that."

She was really put off by me not disclosing this information at our first meet. Fifth Amendment, lady. "I have no obligation to incriminate myself nor volunteer any information freely." She was red in the face, and her movements became more aggressive.

Then she did exactly what I saw in those YouTube videos I checked. She went on the offensive.

"Let me tell you what I think. I think you had something to do with Easton's disappearance. I think you murdered him. I think you disposed of his body. What have you done with Easton? Tell us where his body is. What else did you throw into the lake, Mr. Whitman?"

Her expression was one of anger. Her face blushed red. Her right index finger jabbed a few inches from my chest.

I gave her a look of "what the fuck" and said nothing. I needed her to get this out, and over with. Marg needed this emotional outburst; it's part of their strategy.

I've done a number of debates with people online. Mostly with creationists on evolution, and more than a few times with those who think all climate change is because of humans, and also with leftists on political matters. So I had built up a strategy on debating.

When the opposition of a debate is cornered and can't use evidence, because they have none, they lash out with insults and forceful claims. Marg just did something similar.

My reply to such outburst isn't to counter the argument, but get into the underlying reason such people fall into outburst. It's because they are stumped at what to do next.

I told her that she was fishing, looking for anything because she had not been able to find Easton and explain his disappearance. I admitted that I would not shed a tear if he was found dead. I then put on the guilt, thick, and played the victim. I complained that her bringing Easton back onto my life was an emotional trauma that will take years to get over. No lie there.

I explained to Marg about my wife, and how we won't be spending retirement together, as we had planned. It was tough to get the words out. I hurt deeply to remember our dreams were extinguished by this evil, vile individual.

There was no need to act. I let my emotions go out, mostly because I couldn't hold them back. But I had no choice if I wanted to press my message. Besides, once this was over, the satisfaction would be wonderful to relish for a long, long time.

I was pleased with my performance during the interrogation, I almost convinced myself, even though I had good motive to do Easton in, there was enough doubt they would have no choice but to bypass me.

I need to add one last comment. "So, are you going to arrest me for attempted murder?"

She paused, as if thinking the possibility. I was a bit nervous.

"No. You're free to leave."

What? Holy shit, I pulled it off!

She folded her notebook and got up. Just as she headed out the door the other shoe dropped, "When you get home you'll see we have executed a search warrant. There may be things we've taken." And she left.

That did send a shiver down my spine. But I was confident I had covered my trail.

She never contacted me again. I suspected the protocol was to send my file to the FBI, though I had no idea of that. The fact that, months later, I heard nothing showed my file must have gone cold case. Of course, I wasn't going to call her to pretend to care about what they found out. That would be pushing it too far. They might interpret that as me wanting to see how close they were getting to me.

I had no idea how the rest of the investigation went. She didn't even revisit my wife. I suspected they passed the case off to the FBI, but I never got a call from them either. If the FBI got the file, they would have investigated Easton's apparent flee to Brazil. I pulled it off. The elephant was off my chest.

Well, maybe. I noted a few days after my ordeal in the interrogation room that I was being tailed. I don't go out much. One or two times a week to get food and fuel for the car. I'd been watching, since the very first day Marg visited me, for any hint of a tail. Now I was sure of it. It was a red Nissan, with a man driving it.

Problem was, I had to make a food drop in two days. So one evening I had to spend some time on Google Earth looking for a way to lose the tail. Took several hours, but I figured it out.

When I went on my next food delivery, I'd get the old girl next door to feed my pets. She loves Rug, and my birds. I had already set it up with her to look after them before I started this. I told her I was taking a few days a week to go and watch birds migrating south for the winter. It was a good cover, because I would have to go for two to three days south of Lake Erie. So it would give me a buffer should I need more time after a food drop.

I also made sure I did not get the food from the same stores, that way no one in the checkout would recognize me and see my periodic purchasing of the same things.

Sometimes I would go through Chicago's outskirts to buy the food. Out of the way, but a good way to diversify.

So I figured I'll take this police tail back to Chicago, go into a mall, and backtrack quickly to the car and leave the mall lot before my tail figured out what I had done.

It worked perfectly. I didn't leave completely. I drove across the street, and parked behind a delivery truck. From there I could see the cop looking around. He made a call, likely to Marg. Then off he went, very frustrated I'd bet. Marg was going to go up one side of him and down the other. That was a big load off my shoulders. I could make my food drop.

The day after I got home the old girl next door told me the cop was asking questions, not just her, but others on the street as well. I had to explain what the cops were up to. Not long after I got in the house that cop who was tailing me was at my door asking where I'd been.

"I went bird watching, like I do that every weekend in the fall. So what?" He didn't seem to buy it. He asked how I got away from him at the mall.

"You followed me to the mall?" I said. "Why?"

The cop was quite angry, demanding to know how he missed me.

"Hey, not my fucking fault you messed up. I got in the door and realized I didn't need to go there, and turned around at the door and headed out. Guess you passed me and didn't see me in the crowd."

I could hear him say "bullshit" under his breath as he turned and went to his car. I laughed. Gotcha!

Buggers had my computer though. Hence, I had no way from my home to see Easton. I could go to the library, but not with a tail on me. Now the tail was gone, off I went to the local library so I could quickly check on him a few times.

I did call the Chief of Detectives for several days demanding I get my computer back. I did have legitimate customers who I coded their websites for and I was loosing money, as well as having angry customers.

Finally, on October the eleventh, that cop showed up at the door with my machine. He didn't even say sorry, he just handed me my laptop and left. I was back in business.

I put the X on the date, December the second. I was confident enough that my ordeal with the cops was over so I started a new calendar. I'd heard nothing from the cops since I got my computer back. Today I planed to confront Easton. The day he found out why he was captive.

By the time I got to the farm it was near the end of the day. I couldn't get up the drive, there was too much snow on the ground. I couldn't risk getting stuck. I got my double-barrelled shotgun out of the trunk to load it.

I had to carry the boxes of goodies for Easton the entire three hundred yards to the barn. In the two-foot deep snow it was a struggle. I was exhausted by the time I got to the barn, which I had to dig the doorway free from the snow. It was an overcast day and the light was fading fast.

I turned on the flashlight on the end of my double-barrelled shotgun, unlocked the door, and entered his cage. I shone the light on him. He was a shell of his former self. Dirty, clothes were torn. Water containers and jars littered the floor. His hair was long, and he had a full beard. Of course, I could see this on the webcam, but that was a tiny image. This was real. He really looked like a beaten man. It was a pitiful sight, but I was delighted.

If I were to find an animal chained up and dying like him, I would have to put it out of its misery. But that misery was exactly what I wanted to put him through, as deep as I could. He deserved no less for what he had done to others, not counting myself. His decisions destroyed lives, now I'd destroyed his. I was just sorry it took so long for me to finally get the nerve to pull this off. I'd succeeded, and it felt good.

"So, you're still alive are you," I said.

He looked up in total surprise. His body reanimated, like a Walking Dead zombie, he stumbled to his feet and moved towards me. Perfect, he thought he'd been rescued. Boy was he in for an emotional drop. With the light on him he couldn't see who I was.

"Thank God you found me. Praise the Lord you rescued me!"

"No," I said. Oh, yeah, I could see his joy evaporate into the ceiling.

"Did you get paid you fucker!?" he screeched.

"No. I'm not asking for any money."

"Then what the fuck am I doing here? Who are you?"

"Your saviour."

"My what? My saviour? What the fuck are you taking about?"

"I've come to give you the chance to make peace with yourself."

"Who the fuck are you?" His advance was halted by the chain, like he'd forgotten it was there. "Put the fucking light down and let me see your face."

"Keep guessing," I said. "Who do you think wants you dead?"

"No one, why would anyone want me dead? I've done nothing wrong."

"Nothing wrong!? Well, that really doesn't surprise me. You never did think you did anything wrong."

"WHO ARE YOU?"

Oh, this was so sweet. He had no clue as to who I was or why he was there. He had no control. Perfect. "I told you. But I'll give you a hint. Remember the lawsuit against you?"

"Yeah, how do you... Oh, fuck. It's YOU! You put me in this hellhole. Do you even know how much I have suffered in here, for wha—"

"YOU suffered?" I cut him off, "I've been suffering for ten years because of you."

"How have you suffered? You got money from me. You took MY money!"

Right, a measly two year's pay. That didn't last long. Didn't come close to what I'd lost in pension from the State. Not including the loss of my home value having to sell at a bad time, and losing my wife, my love. He was worse than a magnitude eight earthquake.

"You have no clue, do you? You never did. You emotionally react to situations, you never think before you act. Your actions have impacted how many people? How many people like me have you destroyed their lives? No more. You're done destroying."

That felt great to say. I should have said this to him when I was there, and I realized what he was doing.

"We settled this. Now you want even more from me? You signed an agreement to never come near me again. You will go to jail for this!"

"I think not."

"You want more money, well forget it. You get fuck all from me."

Now the real jab through his heart: "I already got your money."

"You got piddley little from me, not even a year's pay worth."

He was forgetting. "Two years, Shithead. Two years not one, and that was just the beginning."

"You... No more money, you signed an agreement. What do you want?"

Here we go. Now he finds out why he was here. "A confession."

"A what? You're fuckn' CRAZY!"

"It's a free country, I have every right to be crazy."

"Arg!! You're just mind fucking me!"

Excellent, another emotional outburst. Time to prod more. "Have you gone crazy yet?"

"Of course, anyone chained like a mangy dog to a wall would go crazy! Shit!"

"Good, then I have achieved my task. Almost—just one thing left. Your life has been one of control. You try and control everyone you come in contact with..."

"Of course, that's how I built by business, so what?" Easton interjected.

"...no one has been able to control you. Except for my lawsuit. You were totally helpess, and out of control then. It was wonderful to see you flapping like a fish out of water in that courtroom. But it wasn't enough. You didn't learn. So here you are. In a place where you have no control at all. Nothing. Not what you eat, nothin'."

Time to present him with the coup de grâce, his ability to get back some control. Of course, it was an illusion; there was no control on his part, not even his end.

"So, I'm going to force you to get control over one last thing. You're going to make a choice. You're going to confess that you are an evil person. You use people and throw them away like dirt. You confess that your entire life has been a disgrace and a waste and I will fire both barrels into you right now and put you out of your misery. If you don't, I have a bag of food here, enough for three weeks, and a blanket and some clothes. It will have to do you until it runs out. Then you starve.

"Maybe you'll be rescued, maybe you wont. I know you like to take risks, that's how you've gotten ahead. But for once in your life you're going to make a choice. It's your only chance of getting any control back about living and hoping, or dying right now. You're going to admit you are an evil person who does not deserve to live."

He laughed, sitting down he said, "Fuck off."

"So you don't think you did anything wrong."

"I'm not talking to you. You'll be caught. Now get out."

"Suit yourself. I'm going to give you a week to think about this. I'll come back and ask you to choose again."

I put the food on the table, along with the clothing and blanket. Plus something else for him to chew on. "Oh, and by the way, you gave me a great Christmas present. I got the money you stashed in the Caribbean."

I turned the shotgun light off, closed and locked the door. That last comment definitely made him boil. I could hear him screaming and throwing things around.

All the way home, I felt confident, energized, with a smile on my face. In one week, I'd be back for the last time.

PART 4

My grandfather's last will and testament

My grandfather died in Oct of 2041, just shy of his 84th birthday. I didn't see my grandfather at all before I went to university; I was born after he left for the rain forests of Brazil to help endangered parrots.

I was all that was left of my family. My parents were killed during the Great Riots of 2034 while I was at university. Thugs stormed the house stealing everything, including all our family history. They shot both my parents in cold blood. I can't help but wonder; had my great-grandfather's rifle still worked they might have survived. It was a horrible time in our history. Things are still not great. I had a very old Cz85 pistol my husband bought decades ago. I carried it everywhere I went in my bag. Everyone carried a gun those days. It was the only thing keeping crime down.

My grandmother – my grandfather's divorced wife – died a couple years before that from cancer. She used to visit me often from Chicago, but when she got ill, I didn't see her again. We could only converse through video on our computers. My grandfather was devastated that his beloved died, even though they were separated for decades. He couldn't even get away from Brazil for her funeral.

My grandmother told me little about my grandfather, there was nothing in her will about him at all. She was angry with him for a long time. Why she would never say, other than she left him.

All I had as a connection to my grandfather as I grew up was the yearly birthday card, Christmas card, and paying my education fund. Thousands each year, more than enough for me to get my PhD during the toughest economic times in society, worse than the Great Depression.

It always puzzled me how he could afford it. I suspected he used his entire pension for my education, leaving nothing for himself. I was about to find out otherwise.

Even with so little contact, he inspired me greatly. I knew about his parrots, and that he went off to save them in the wilds of the rain forest. I didn't know the real reason why he left; I was soon to find that out as well.

I wanted to study parrots, get my degree and do what he did. But the economics of the time prevented it. The entire world economy collapsed 31 years ago and things had deteriorated until about ten years ago. With the climate finally warming from thirty years of global cooling, things were slowly improving. Government was restored, the military restored order around the country. The economy was actually, albeit slowly, recovering. But a lot of people weren't around for the recovery.

It all started in the Middle East. Those countries had to import food for a very fast growing population. But their credit ran out. Hundreds of millions starved to death over there. The effects snowballed infecting countries in the Europian Union as their debt crushed their economies. The cancer quickly spread to North America.

Food was of vital importance to our own survival. So, instead I got my PhD in agriculture, and subsequently I worked in the food production industry, a vital and noble occupation those early days of the recovery, called The New Rebirth. Some called the years previous The Great Cleansing. It was nothing of the sort. Those eco-fascists, as I called them, must have been sick in the head. Growing up in those years was a nightmare.

I did meet my grandfather, much to his surprise. Not needing to work over the summers because of his funding me, I decided to do what he had been doing for two years before my birth. I went to help with parrot research and conservation. I just had to meet my grandfather.

My first visit was a complete surprise. He had no prior knowledge I was coming. That was May of 2022.

He didn't look like what I expected. He was old, very old looking. Life weighed heavy on him. He was all white, not what the pictures I had seen of him from the past.

We hit it off. I was, after all, his only grandchild.

He still had his cockatoo, though he too was very old. Every day I was there that cockatoo was on his shoulder, or very near by in a tree.

I managed to only make the pilgrimage for six summers, as by 2028 flight travel collapsed as the oil crisis went from bad to worse. That's when the rioting started all over the world. Thus, I had no way of getting there except to walk. A bit too far from California.

We did write, and even sent Internet videos. But then two years ago, it stopped. Emails from the research station said he suffered a stroke. They were giving him the best care they could. I could do nothing. I'd never felt so helpless.

Today I got a call from a lawyer. He informed me my grandfather died of heart failure and the lawyer was in possession of my grandfather's last will and testament. My appointment was for 3:30pm.

The meeting was short, barely fifteen minutes. All he did was hand me an envelope and I signed a paper. I was out the door. Just like that, it was all over. Here one moment, gone the next.

On the bus home – cars were a luxury those days – I opened the envelope, unwilling to wait until I got in my apartment.

There was only one thing in the envelope: a safety deposit box key. Attached to the key was a tag. "Chase Manhattan Bank of Chicago" on one side, on the other "You must get the contents." The postmarked stamp from Brazil was two years ago. He knew he was dying.

Right, nice, I had to go to Chicago. How the hell was I going to afford to do that? Travel was damned expensive. That's why few traveled those days.

When I got home, I discussed the situation with my husband. I told him there was something important about this key. He agreed, reluctantly, to let me take the two-week trip. Train travel was the only way one can get to far away places.

Next was to convince my boss. I was owed several weeks' holidays, which I had yet to take, but this was a busy time. He agreed I could go as long as I took my laptop and worked on the train. Yes, even in that brutal economic times we were in, the Internet still worked. It was a lifeline. Literally.

It took me five days to get to Chicago. Like other cities, there were no taxis, fuel was too expensive and rationed for more important purposes, so I had to take the "L" and walk to the bank.

The manager took me into a small cubical, and I handed him the key. He returned with the safety deposit box. I opened it. There were only two things in it, a brown envelope and a small box. The box was heavy, very heavy.

"And there is this," the manager said as he handed me a paper. It was an account at this bank. It had almost one million dollars in it!

"It's in gold," the manager said.

Gold? How did my grandfather accumulate so much gold? Did he have forethought enough to not have worthless old US dollars?

"It weighs just over one hundred pounds," he said.

"That's one million?" I asked.

"In today's new dollars, yes. In old dollars thirty years ago, when your grandfather set up the account, it was much more."

"How did my grandfather afford all this?"

"Let's see..." the manager said looking through the account papers. "Well, it seems he transferred the money over some twenty years, a bit at a time, ten thousand every month, and bought gold. Oh, this is interesting. He stopped just before the economic crash. Your grandfather was one smart man. I'd bet he put his retirement into gold to weather the economic storm. Smart indeed. People lost everything in that collapse."

Wow. I wondered, did he plan to come home from Brazil and retire on this money?

The manager left.

I opened the box. In it were three one-pound bars of solid gold. It was so shiny, perfectly reflective yellow metal. I was awestruck.

I opened the envelope. A bound manuscript was inside. It was hand written. It had a one-word title: "Confession".

I read it right there, all thirty pages, unable to put it down. It was written last year, directly to me. Here is it in its entirety.

Confession
By Edward J. Whitman
Jan. 1, 2038

Dear Jossie:

You deserve to know the truth about me.

I murdered Nick Easton, and I never got caught.

First, I need to explain why. Easton was a very nasty person. He was the most selfish person I have ever come across. He thought nothing of enticing people from secure jobs, promising them just enough, but not too much to be too good to be true, to work for him. He would work these people hard, pay them reasonably, make a fortune from their work, and then throw them to the streets.

I know for a fact this was devastating to the former workers and their families.

I was also enticed, and fired when no longer needed.

My job was IT manager. I wrote software specific for his business. In fact, without my software he would never have gotten his business off the ground.

At that time I worked for the State of Illinois as an IT manager. I maintained databases and wrote software for the State. I also did work on the side for small businesses. It was a boom time for IT people, and I was part of it.

Pay at the State was not that great. It was OK, with a good pension, and other benefits. But I was as far as I could go there. No more advancement was possible.

Easton was so impressed with my work he offered me several thousand on the spot to create a database and write the programs. He paid more once it was done.

For the following years, I wrote more software, and did data analysis on client data he was obtaining. I wrote the analysis, and he would present that to the clients. They paid handsomely for this as at the time we were unique in our abilities. No one was close to us in analytical and comprehensive detail.

His business took off, and I was well paid.

It got to the point where my inability to be at his office during business hours was holding back projects. He wanted me full time. He pestered me for months.

I refused because I would take a hit on my pension with the State.

He got so desperate he offered to put half a million in a special account, which I could use to pay into a retirement fund, which he said would make up for my lost pension. He also guaranteed me work until I was 65.

To work for Easton full time would mean I'd have to live in Chicago, I moved that summer. Though for the rest of the year I commuted to my State job, while working at Easton's in the evening and weekends.

I had to do that for two years until I became eligible for early retirement from the State.

I retired, and worked for Easton full time starting in 1993.

Things went very well, the business was expanding, he was hiring new people to do projects.

However, people were hired, and fired, on a regular basis. He would entice people from other companies we did projects for. They would come and work for Easton, then he'd let them go after a year or two. Why? Because he felt they couldn't make him enough money.

I know that for a fact, because he said so. Not to me, but I over heard it through my office door.

He knew what he was doing. He knew he would bring people from other jobs to only let them go after a year or so.

I should have seen the handwriting on the wall, but my analytical skills were so important to the health of the company, I figured he'd keep me, if not because of loyalty, but because without my skills he could not continue to function. Naïve? Yes.

By 2000 I had pretty much completed automating the entire office. Projects now could be completed in record time, because, literally, once the data was in the system, a single push of the button allowed the statistics to drop into Excel.

This took years to happen only because it took years for the programming languages to become powerful enough, and the computers to become powerful enough, and hard drive capacity large enough, for us to do the work this way.

One day he walked into my office with his father, who was the CFO, and fired me on the spot. The reason he gave was I screwed up an account and a client was suing him.

I later found out it was a lie. No one was suing him. It turned out he wanted some woman in my position, and he had to get me out somehow. So he framed me.

The project he claimed I screwed up was fine. It took me time to pack up my stuff, and in that period I checked on the account. Here is the best guess I have as to what happened.

Data had been entered and analysis done and sent to the client two months prior to that day. The week before he fired me he asked me to do a rerun of the data. Didn't make sense, no new data, obviously same result in the analysis. But he demanded it. So I reran it.

I checked the records of the project, and indeed there were too many records. Someone had reentered previous data. To add those dupe records, the program would prompt to make sure you indeed wanted to add a duplicate record. Someone ignored the prompts.

I was not told of this extra data entry. No one came and asked if it was OK to do so. That was the normal protocol.

Easton and I had quite the argument about why he fired me. He even offered money to leave with the stipulation I not pursue him further.

I sued Easton and his company, and he lost that suit in court. I was awarded two years severance. That was not good enough.

To top it off, every time I tried to get a job, Easton would black-ball me and I wouldn't get hired. My life of working, what I enjoyed so much, which was programming, was gone. No one would hire me. I was way too old. The economy was worsening, and companies wanted new kids. I was devastated.

You know your Gran and I separated. This is why. We lost our home, we lost a lot of our savings. All I had left was my father's home and my meagre pension to live on. I was all alone except for my animals.

It got so bad, I actually planned to actively kill him. I even bought a handgun illegally. That's how depressed and devastated I was. I even planned to make a radio controlled airplane fitted with a rifle barrel and scope. Both plans weren't acted on.

I did have one in. I'd often have to use Remote Desktop to get into the company server from home to do work. I suspect he had no clue what that was, because for 2 months I could still log in.

That allowed me to plant a program that would give me total login ability even if I was no longer normally able to do so. It was a back door.

Thus for ten years I was able to follow his company, and all files on his personal machine when it was connected to the network.

I downloaded important financial files, including his spreadsheet he used to keep track of his side business. Easton used a shell company to bill his business. He then funnelled that money into an offshore account.

I had the account number and the password to get in.

It took about 10 years to accumulate, which by that time he had some five million dollars in it. The bank was in the Cayman Islands. It was time to act.

I set up a plan to take the money. But that wasn't good enough. Easton needed to be punished big time.

Jossie, this is exactly what I did.

I practiced this two previous times to make sure it would work and get any bugs ironed out.

First step was to take my normal trip to the Canadian Rockies in September. That way my yearly two week camping trip in the wilderness looked perfectly routine.

In 2010 I came home immediately after arriving by train to Kamloops. I came back across the boarder as a different person.

It took some doing, but I managed to get fake ID and passports.

I came home and rented a van. I drove to Easton's building in the evening waiting for him to come out to go home. I was parked beside his car.

Soon as he showed up to unlock his door, I stunned him with a taser. I managed to tie him up, and get him into the van where I gave him a drug to put him out for the drive to the barn. That's the barn your Grandmother owned. She willed it to you. It's yours.

I chained him to the wall in a horse stall, and left.

Next I had to take on Easton's identity. I drove his car to Houston, Texas. I rented a flat bed truck, put his car on it and drove out of the city. I found an isolated spot on a deserted road, torched his car, and returned the truck to Houston.

I then took a flight to Florida under a different name. From there, I took a flight to the Cayman Islands under his name using his credit card. I needed to plant a trail for the cops to follow.

Easton had never visited the bank there, in fear of getting caught I suspect. I showed up and transferred all the money to a bank account in Brazil.

I then took a flight, again using his card as a trail, to Brazil that day.

Once there, I changed identities again to a fake, got back onto a plane and flew to O'Hare. I went to the barn to feed him, then flew to BC. I took a train back to Kamloops to resume my camping trip. I returned home under my own name.

Easton was my hostage, my captive. He had to be put in a situation where he had no control over anything, completely against his nature to want control over everything for his own personal gain.

I fed him once a week, and waited until December to confront him.

He was a shell of his former self. He was exactly where I wanted him to be.

I gave him the choice to admit he was a failure as a human being, and I'd shoot him dead right there. Or leave him to starve, or maybe get rescued. He chose the latter. I expected nothing less.

I returned a week after that ultimatum, he was still defiant. He would never admit his guilt. So I left never to return. If he wasn't rescued, his body will still be there, Jossie.

Yes, cops did visit me, and even likely suspected me at his disappearance. But they stopped after a couple months. So it looked like my diversion worked. They think he absconded with company money to Brazil, likely with another woman.

I waited about some six months after that and finally sold everything and left for Brazil. The money I got from Easton was used to help fund research into parrot conservation. Some of it funded your education.

I'm old now, and close to death. I'm so sorry I have to put this on your shoulders. But I felt it my duty to tell you. I actually feel bad about putting this on you. I hope you can forgive me.

Everything I have will go to you. I'm glad we had those few times to be together. I wish I could have been there for you during those bad years. But I knew you'd make it.

I'm so proud of you, and I love you very much.

Signed,
Ed Whitman.

Wow. I was flabbergasted. My grandfather kidnapped and killed a former employer some thirty years ago, and he never got caught. I new my grandmother owned a small farm near Chicago. Technically it was mine. She willed it to me. But with long-range transportation a rare event, especially to get out to a distant farm, I never made the trek to the property. It never reverted to the county, so somehow property taxes were being paid, though few actually could afford to pay property taxes. Most local governments, even state governments, went bankrupt years ago. Now I know who paid for the property taxes. My grandfather.

But, like, wow again. There was a body in the old barn!

I doubted the police investigator was still working, likely not even alive. But what could I do? Do I go to the cops with this? If I do will I lose the gold? That kind of money will do us for life. Those thoughts raced through my mind. That much money would do my twins for their lives. What the fuck to do?

I sat there, until the bank manager returned and asked if I needed any more time.

"No," I said. "How can I take the gold with me?"

"It's in crates. I'll get one of the boys to bring it out to you."

They brought it out, five boxes of twenty pounds each. One hundred pounds of gold! Hell, I weighted just over that myself!

"How am I going to get this to the train?" I said to the manager.

"Always willing to help a valued customer. My assistant will get the van and take you to the station."

A van? He had a van?! Wow, that was rare. Guess they did need one.

We were the only vehicle on the road from the bank to the train station. I made sure they got it on the first train back west. I wasn't heading home.

I asked at the station where the police headquarters was. I could walk it and be there before dark.

I took the confession with me. It's been so many years that the case must have been closed. Yes, even in this economic depression, with murders at an all time high, with few investigations due to lack of resources, I felt it was my duty to take the confession and close the book on this murder. It's almost as if my grandfather wanted this to get to the police. Why else the confession? He could have taken this to his grave in Brazil.

I had my gold safe from the cops, so what would it hurt to tell them? Everyone involved was long gone anyway. Not like anyone was going to be arrested.

I had to wait hours at the police station before someone from homicide would talk to me. Finally, at three in the morning, a thin looking man in his forties with long hair and scrubby beard came into the room.

"Hi, Joanne, I'm Investigator Ralph Wolfe, what can I do for you?"

"You had a case here some thirty years ago, a missing persons."

"Ma'am, we've had a million of those, so what?"

"The person was murdered and my grandfather did it. Here is his confession. I got it today from his safety deposit box at the bank." I handed it to him.

He read it fully. Scratched his beard a number of times, stopping a few times to drink from his cup of water. Finally, he put the bound papers down and said, "Is this all of it?"

"Yes." That was a lie. There was nothing in the confession about the gold at the bank.

"Where's your grandfather now, dead I guess?"

"Yes, he's buried in the Brazilian rain forest."

He muttered a bit which I couldn't comprehend. He flipped back through some of the pages, pausing at places to re-read. "I'll be back." He left the room.

Returning about an hour later he said, "You have a place to stay?"

"Not yet, I was hoping to head back to Bakersfield tonight."

"Not today you aren't. You're stayin' right here."

"Am I under arrest?"

"No, a person of interest for now."

He left the room again.

About three hours later, totally bored to tears and getting worried, a female cop came in and said, "Go to a hotel, here's a voucher for one night's stay. Come back some time in the afternoon. Go get some sleep, honey."

I did manage to call my husband and tell him I'd be a few more days than I had hoped, and to call work for me. He wasn't too happy with that. I didn't tell him about the gold—not yet. Didn't tell him about the murder either. I told him there were complications with my mother's farm. That wasn't a lie. When I got home, I'd explain it.

Man, was I tired. But before I drifted off, I thought about the situation, and that gold. I got to wonder if maybe we could move to the farm and grow crops for a living. Or sell the farm. *Wonder how much I could get for it...*

I slept the whole time.

I returned around 4pm. I was back in the same interrogation room again. And, of course, the waiting. Finally, officer Wolfe came in with a bundle of papers in folders.

"This case was closed decades ago as a missing persons and fraud. The detective was..." He looked through the reports. "Oh, Marg Cunningham. I remember her. I was just a rookie at the time, but she busted a big murder case. Some fat real estate wheeler-dealer guy got popped. She cracked the case wide open. Brought a whole mob family down."

"Is she still around?"

"No. She died some ten, maybe fifteen years ago. So, according to this, it was claimed Easton ran off to Brazil with his company's money, likely with someone and not his wife. But Marg's notes here says she thought Ed Whitman did it. That's your grandfather?"

"Yes."

"Interesting. Now this confession tells us Easton was murdered by your grandfather and even where the body is."

He paused. "Damn, Marg was right after all. Too bad she never lived to find the truth. So, since your grandfather murdered him, did he take that money? I see nothing in this confession saying where the money went."

I was in a bind there. I needed to say it in such a way as to not lie, but not tell the truth either.

"It says he devoted his life to parrots. I would guess he gave it to them."

The officer huffed, and muttered something inaudible. Paused, then said, "Likely lost in the economic crash anyway. OK, let's go, we're going to confirm this right now."

Another car ride! Wow, what a treat that was. I had no idea where the farm was, but Wolfe had looked up the title and they had directions. It took us three hours to get there, and it was starting to get dark.

The property was well over grown. The house was nothing but a collapsed pile of rotted lumber. The barn was well shrunken with large trees growing throughout it. There were other cops there, the state police. They had to chainsaw their way into the lower level of the barn.

Soon as we arrived, a state officer told Wolfe that a body was found in the basement, chained to a wall, just as the confession said. Of course, it was only bones.

"There's no indications of gunshot," she said to Wolfe. "Looks like our victim starved to death. Guess the rats had a good feast."

Easton never admitted he was a psychopath. My grandfather dished out justice.

The Author's previous novels are available on Amazon, Kobo, Barnes & Noble, Chapters/Indigo, as well as in the Apple iBookstore.

Blinding White Flash

"There are too many excellent elements of "Blinding White Flash" to list in one review. The author, J. Richard Wakefield, has created a masterpiece about the lengths ordinary citizens will go to in order to defend their country from foreign invasion. While many books in the military/war/action-adventure genre are thrilling to read, "Blinding White Flash" thrusts the reader into the heart of war with all of its pain, bloodshed as well as heroism and valor. Wakefield gets down to the nitty gritty of the conflict between the force made up largely of Canadian volunteers who give blood, sweat and tears to stop the Chinese government from seizing Canada and its resources. It's obvious that Mr. Wakefield has a strong knowledge not only of weaponry but military history and strategy as well. The battle scenes are gripping and spellbinding at the same time: the intensity, the hardships the men endure are all captured.

The tone of "Blinding White Flash" truly fits the description of war: bloody, traumatizing, at times heart-wrenching. No punches are pulled here. The characters in the book display the type of selfless valor and bravery that has exemplified the Canadian soldier from the trenches of Vimy Ridge to Afghanistan.

In my opinion, "Blinding White Flash" should be either a blockbuster movie or a television series. In some ways, this larger-than-life story resembles Leo Tolstoy's iconic tale of love and fighting War and Peace. Like the Russian soldiers who fought valiantly to drive Napoleon's forces from their land (and did 150 years later when Hitler invaded the Soviet Union) the Canadian fighters are often outgunned and outnumbered by superior Chinese forces. Also, they use the brutal cold of the Canadian winter as a very effective weapon against the invaders.

From start-to-finish, "Blinding White Flash" holds the reader in its grip and doesn't let go."

Blinding White Flash: Invasion

"It's hard to believe that Invasion is even better than the almost flawless war story Blinding White Flash. Blinding White Flash: Invasion has a bit different tone to it than the original book.

Invasion starts in British Columbia. Groups of Canadian soldiers and civilians are preparing to defend Canada from tens of thousands of Chinese troops that are landing on the west coast. The action moves inland to the BC interior and onwards into Alberta.

While Blinding White Flash is a masterpiece of thrilling action sequences and a strong storyline that features amazing characters, Invasion is much more intense. The sequel delves more into the politics behind the conflict that is ravaging much of the world. In same ways, the book is a commentary of the unstable times we live in globally.

The author has intensely-researched every fine detail of the book to make every bit of the story factual and even believable. Even the villains, namely the Chinese general, are not merely one-dimensional characters but have strong and weak points, as well as reasons for doing what they do.

Blinding White Flash: Invasion is a mind-blowing read that is phenomenal from start to finish."

The Cunningham Arrests

(Available October 2015)

In this sequel to **The Barn**, Marg Cunningham must investigate how her father obtained hundreds of thousands of dollars, which she found in her mother's home.

Expecting to have a two-week vacation, she is ordered back to the Division. She is transferred to homicide to investigate the recent murder of a witness she interviewed for the case of missing Nick Easton.

In this fast pace, emotional roller coaster ride, she discovers the reality of being a homicide detective, which severely challenges her worldview.